THE ILLINOIS DETECTIVE AGENCY:
THE CASE OF THE MISSING CHILDREN

T0244191

THE ILLINOIS DETECTIVE AGENCY: THE CASE OF THE MISSING CHILDREN

BOOK 4

AL LAMANDA WRITING AS ETHAN J. WOLFE

WHEELER PUBLISHING
A part of Gale, a Cengage Company

Copyright © 2023 by Ethan J. Wolfe
Wheeler Publishing, a part of Gale, a Cengage Company.

ALL RIGHTS RESERVED

Wheeler Publishing Large Print Softcover Western.
The text of this Large Print edition is unabridged.
Other aspects of the book may vary from the original edition.
Set in 16 pt. Plantin.

LIBRARY OF CONGRESS CIP DATA ON FILE.
CATALOGUING IN PUBLICATION FOR THIS BOOK
IS AVAILABLE FROM THE LIBRARY OF CONGRESS.

ISBN-13: 978-1-4328-9583-9 (softcover alk. paper)

Published in 2023 by arrangement with Alfred J. Lamanda.

Printed in the United States of America
1 2 3 4 5   27 26 25 24 23

THE ILLINOIS DETECTIVE AGENCY: THE CASE OF THE MISSING CHILDREN

PROLOGUE

"Charles, we have to go home," Miss Potts said. "We've neglected the office for weeks now. It's time."

They were sitting on a bench in a prominent park, watching children play under the watchful eyes of nannies and mothers.

As he puffed on a cigar, Porter said, "I know it."

"We can assign Duffy and Cavill to the case and . . ."

"Miss Potts, that man hiding in those trees over there, see him?" Porter said.

"Where?" Miss Potts said.

Porter took binoculars from a pocket and zoomed in on the man in the trees. "It's him. It's Valdez," Porter said.

"What?" Miss Potts said.

"Valdez. Right there in those trees," Porter said.

"Oh my God," Miss Potts said.

Porter stood. "Alert the deputies in the

park," he said and ran toward the man in the trees.

"Charles, stop!" Miss Potts shouted.

By the time Porter reached the trees, Valdez was gone. There was a well-worn path, and Porter ran along the path, drawing his .32 revolver from the shoulder holster as he ran.

Not as young as he once was, Porter was winded after a hundred yards or so, but he kept running, hoping to gain sight of Valdez up ahead.

Porter never saw the knife that was suddenly stuck in his gut.

As he dropped to his knees, Porter caught sight of Valdez as he stood there watching.

By the time Miss Potts and several deputies caught up to Porter, he was on the ground in a pool of blood with a large knife protruding from his stomach.

He was still alive but fading quickly.

Miss Potts, tears streaming down his face, knelt beside Porter and cradled his head.

"You old fool," she said. "Why didn't you wait?"

"It was him. Valdez," Porter said.

"Be still. Don't talk," Miss Potts said.

"I haven't much time," Porter said. "In the office safe. My will. Read it."

"Charles," Miss Potts said as Porter closed

his eyes and went still.

In accordance with Porter's will, he wished a small, private ceremony without fanfare.

Sato made the trip to Springfield for the church service and funeral. No one questioned why he did so or seemed to mind.

The day after the funeral, Duffy, Cavill, Goodluck, Miss Potts, Sato, and Quill and Harvey, as well as several other agents, met in the meeting room at the office.

Porter's lawyer read the will. Miss Potts was made office manager and given ten percent controlling interest. Duffy, Cavill, and Goodluck were also given ten percent controlling interest.

All other agents were given between two and five percent.

Duffy was promoted to director of the agency, with Cavill as vice president.

After the lawyer left the office, Duffy turned to Miss Potts and said, "Miss Potts, tell us what Mr. Porter was working on."

CHAPTER ONE

James Duffy stared out the window of the office that once belonged to Charles Porter, the founder of the Illinois Detective Agency. As of one week ago, the office now belonged to him.

Except that he wasn't sure he wanted it in the wake of Porter's murder in Dallas, Texas.

On the desk was a box of Porter's Cuban cigars. He picked one up, bit off the tip, and lit it with a wood match.

It was still very difficult for Duffy to believe Porter was gone. Although Porter was in his mid-sixties, he was still a bull of a man with a dizzying intellect, and the man never stopped working. His capacity for work was incredible.

That work ethic ultimately led to his doom.

Duffy turned to Porter's workbench. He had been working on so many things to advance forensics and science. He was organizing a catalogue of criminals by photo and description that he called a mug book. He was testing various inks and powders to develop a fingerprint kit. He was trying to get law enforcement through Congress to keep records on ballistics at a time when most people had never even heard the term.

When Porter founded the agency in 1848, he worked as a stock detective with the sole purpose of protecting cattle from rustlers. The west was barely settled back then, and those with the guts to start ranches had to battle Indians and rustlers alike, more often than not losing cattle and their lives in the process.

Men like Porter kept the ranges safe so the ranches could grow and feed an ever expanding population back east.

And now he was dead. Murdered at the hands of a child slaver named King Valdez out of Mexico.

At last count, one hundred and seventeen children had been abducted by Valdez's band of slavers, but that's only those they were aware of. The actual number could be twice that or more.

Valdez had a system in place. Target children of the wealthy, between the ages of eight to twelve. Children of the wealthy tended to be healthier and stronger than children of the poor. They lived in larger cities and tended to have nannies. Nannies who took them to parks to play.

Valdez and his people targeted the parks. The end result was missing children. How many was an unanswered question. Boys were sold for labor. Girls had a far worse fate.

While Duffy was chasing down the man who murdered his ex-girlfriend, Porter took it upon himself to investigate Valdez, a decision that resulted in his murder.

A knock came on the office door.

"Yes," Duffy said.

The door opened and Miss Potts entered. "Everybody is here, Jim," she said.

Porter's will had made Miss Potts, his personal assistant for a dozen years, a full partner.

Duffy nodded and followed Miss Potts to the meeting room. Assembled at the table were Jack Cavill, Joseph Goodluck, Harvey, Quill, and Sato.

Sato, a Japanese engineer they rescued several months ago when they were tracking the killer of Duffy's ex-girlfriend, had decided to stick around for a while.

Cavill smoked a cigar. Goodluck smoked his well-worn pipe.

Miss Potts went for the coffeepot in the

lunchroom and filled a cup for everybody at the table.

"How long are we going to sit on our hands, Jim?" Cavill said. "Valdez could be halfway to South America by now."

"He isn't," Duffy said. "Quill, Harvey, what have you been able to find out?"

"We spent the last five days collecting data from police departments, sheriffs, and marshals around the country," Harvey said. "More than twenty new cases of missing children have been reported since . . . Mr. Porter's death."

"Specifics?" Duffy said.

"Saint Louis and San Francisco," Quill said.

"Two large cities separated by a thousand miles," Duffy said.

"Well, why are we sitting on our asses then?" Cavill said.

Duffy turned to Miss Potts. "I sent telegrams to Washington, to the Justice Department. They will do everything they can to locate Valdez, but they aren't equipped for such an undertaking. US Marshals are spread thin, and the army isn't qualified for this kind of work. Miss Potts?"

Miss Potts held up a telegram and said, "We have been authorized by the Justice Department to hunt down and bring to justice King Valdez by any means possible, and to end his organization."

"And all the missing children?" Sato said.

"Once we have Valdez, the Justice Department will do what it can to locate and return them," Duffy said.

"You know what that means," Cavill said. "They will give him a sweet deal in exchange for the kids."

"Possibly," Duffy said.

"Likely is more like it," Cavill said.

"So how are we handling this?" Harvey said.

"I've sent telegrams to the police in San Francisco and Saint Louis telling them to expect us inside the week," Duffy said.

"Quill and Harvey, you will travel to Saint Louis and meet with the police," Duffy said. "Miss Potts will give you the particulars."

"When do we leave?" Quill said.

"Tomorrow if possible," Duffy said. "Jack, you, Joseph, and Mr. Sato head out to San Francisco."

"What about you?" Cavill said.

"Miss Potts and I are going to Washington to meet with the Justice Department," Duffy said. "Go home and pack and report back here tomorrow morning to draw tickets and expense money."

Everybody at the table stood.

15

"Mr. Sato, a moment please," Duffy said. Duffy and Sato went to Duffy's office.

"Mr. Sato, I'm sending you with Jack and Goodluck to San Francisco so you can meet your family," Duffy said. "I'm grateful for your help on the trail but it's about time you returned to your family."

"I wish to see this through to the end," Sato said. "My family will understand."

"Are you sure?" Duffy said.

"I never knew how boring designing railroad bridges was until you and Mr. Cavill came to my aid and we rode together," Sato said. "I believe it is far more important that I help you find this Valdez person and stop what he is doing to those children than to build another bridge over a stream."

"All right," Duffy said. "You'll draw pay like any other agent on the job."

Sato nodded.

"Be ready to leave tomorrow," Duffy said.

Chapter Two

In his house a few blocks from the office, Duffy poured a drink of whiskey and packed for a week in Washington.

After packing, he took his drink to the window and looked out at the darkening streets of Springfield.

Porter had many opportunities to relocate the office to Chicago, but he disliked large cities and saw no reason to move. Springfield was where the company was born and Springfield was where it would stay.

Doctor Kathy Bodine, whom Duffy had met in Fort Jones a while back, entered the bedroom.

"Dinner is ready, Jim," she said.

Kathy was close to Duffy's age, tall with blond hair and soft, hazel colored eyes.

Duffy followed Kathy to the small dining room off the kitchen. She had made a roasted chicken with potatoes and carrots.

They sat at the table.

"You'll leave for Washington tomorrow?" Kathy said.

"Noon train."

"Do you still want me here?" Kathy said.

"More than ever," Duffy said. "We can live on the second floor while you set up your practice on the first, just like we talked about."

"I applied for a staff position at Springfield General for two days a week," Kathy said. "Leaving me three days a week for private practice."

"When will you know?" Duffy said.

"A couple of weeks," Kathy said. "In the meantime, I will go back to Fort Jones for all my medical equipment."

"I'm going to have a telegraph line brought to the house," Duffy said. "Do you know Morse code?"

"No, but I made it through medical school, so I think I can learn," Kathy said.

"I have a book on Morse code you can study on the ride back to Fort Jones," Duffy said.

"Jim, am I going to be Mrs. Kathy Duffy or Kathy Bodine?" Kathy said.

"We'll make it official as soon as you return," Duffy said.

It was a warm night and they took coffee to the balcony in the bedroom. The balcony

18

was large enough for a small table and two chairs.

"Jim, I know how sad you are over Mr. Porter," Kathy said. "I want you to know I will stand by you, no matter what you decide."

"Finding Valdez means a lot to me," Duffy said.

"I know," Kathy said.

"After it's done, I promise you we'll have a good life together," Duffy said.

"I'm going to hold you to that," Kathy said.

"I hope you do," Duffy said.

CHAPTER THREE

Cavill packed for the trip to San Francisco and opened his gun safe. He always wore his custom-made Colt revolver that fit the custom-made holster like a glove, but he had several spare handguns in the safe for emergency use.

He selected a three-year-old Colt Peacemaker with a brown leather holster and took it to the second bedroom where Sato had been staying.

Sato had borrowed a suitcase and had it packed on the bed.

"Sato, wear this," Cavill said. "An agent can't go around unarmed while on a case."

Sato took the Colt and looked it over. "It is a beautiful weapon," he said. "I shall take very good care of it."

"You'll need a Winchester," Cavill said. "Come to my safe. I have three extra ones."

Sato followed Cavill to his bedroom and looked in the safe. He selected the Winchester Model 75.

"I know you know that fancy Japanese fighting, but can you handle a gun and rifle?" Cavill said.

"I can handle both with accuracy," Sato said.

"Fair enough," Cavill said. "Let's get something to eat."

"I shall cook," Sato said.

"I have a better idea," Cavill said.

Thirty minutes later, Cavill and Sato cut into thick steaks at a restaurant near his house.

"Very good," Sato said.

"I have a question for you," Cavill said.

"Yes?"

"Are you any good at letter writing?" Cavill said. "I mean the romantic type of letter."

"You have a girl?" Sato said.

"A very pretty one," Cavill said. "And she's been patient with me so far, but me going away again, I just don't know."

"Tell her the circumstances," Sato said. "She'll understand."

"That's where I need the help," Cavill said. "I'm terrible when it comes to expressing my feelings."

Sato smiled. "I will help you after dinner," he said.

"Not too mushy," Cavill said. "I don't want her to think I've gone soft."

"No, not too mushy," Sato said with a grin.

CHAPTER FOUR

Miss Potts ate dinner alone in her apartment and tried very hard not to cry.

She cried anyway.

She had held Porter in her arms as he took his final breath. Even then, he was thinking of her and the others.

She had always been a fair-minded person with no hatred in her heart, but she wanted to find Valdez and watch Jack Cavill beat him to death. If not that, she'd take a front row seat at his hanging, where she would eat popcorn and take delight in watching him swing.

After dinner, she packed for the trip to Washington. They would be there at least a week, so she needed many changes of clothes.

Once the packing was done, she opened her briefcase to check the tickets and train schedule.

She and Mr. Duffy were booked on the

noon train to Washington.

Odd how she'd rarely called him Mr. Duffy when Porter was alive. She always called him Jim or James, but now that he was left in charge, Mr. Duffy seemed to fit better.

The last item she packed was the .32 caliber revolver she inherited from Porter. It was a fine weapon that he always carried when not officially on a case. If he needed to go out west, he used his Colt Peacemaker, but otherwise he used the .32.

Sometimes, if he was overly busy, Porter would ask her to clean the weapon for him, so she knew the workings well. She broke it down, cleaned and oiled it, then loaded it and put it in the handbag she would take to Washington.

She wouldn't need it, not in Washington and not traveling with Mr. Duffy, but it was like carrying a tiny piece of Porter around with her.

With nothing left to pack, Miss Potts poured a glass of sherry and went to her bedroom window for some cool night air.

She didn't want to and she tried hard not to, but she found herself crying again.

"Oh, get it together," Miss Potts said aloud.

Chapter Five

Joseph Goodluck had been many things in his fifty years of life. His father was Comanche but his mother was Mexican. He was raised full Comanche, although his mother insisted he also learn Spanish.

He was raised to be a warrior and killed his first white man when he was just thirteen. When he was fifteen, the white army killed his father. He fought in the great Comanche Wars, but the army was too large and powerful to defeat, and he found himself living on a reservation in New Mexico.

There he learned to speak English and French.

Willing to do anything to get off the reservation, Goodluck volunteered to be an army scout. The army was only too willing to have a scout who not only knew the land and the Indian people, but who spoke four languages to boot.

He scouted for many armies and many

commanding officers, including General Crook. He scouted for the famous Lieutenant Gatewood and helped capture Geronimo when he went on the warpath.

The army paid him well. He married a young Comanche girl and they had a child. Both were taken early by smallpox disease.

He did other things for the army as well. He drove cattle for their beef and became a fair hand. He learned to brand and became good at that as well.

Sometimes, when busy enough, he almost didn't miss his wife.

General Crook picked Goodluck for a special assignment a while back. Large numbers of cattle disappeared from Montana and neighboring states and territories. Goodluck was to work undercover and infiltrate the cattle thieves and work as one of them.

It took quite a while to establish his cover, but he finally found himself working as a brander for the large group of rustlers.

Not known at the time was that the Illinois Detective Agency had been hired by the governor of Montana for the same purpose. Goodluck crossed paths with Duffy and Cavill, and they worked together to apprehend the rustlers or, in this case, kill them.

Afterward, Charles Porter offered him a job at the agency as an agent.

Porter was the most fair-minded man Goodluck had ever known. Porter gave responsibility to Goodluck that even the army never did. Porter assigned him the task of assembling what Porter called the "mug book." He also helped Porter test powders and ink for fingerprinting, something most in law enforcement never even heard of. Ballistics was another project of Porter's that Goodluck helped with.

It seemed to Goodluck that Porter never saw his Comanche/Mexican skin or his long hair, but rather his talents and intelligence.

In his small apartment near the office, Goodluck packed for the trip and then filled a small glass with whiskey.

He lifted the glass and said, "Rest well, my friend," and took a small sip.

CHAPTER SIX

Goodluck met Cavill and Sato at the company stable adjacent to the office at seven o'clock in the morning. Porter had a stable of a dozen horses for his agents.

Goodluck kept his own horse there as well.

Cavill rode Blue, a large horse suited for Cavill's size. The man stood six-foot-four in his bare feet and weighed a muscular two hundred and fifty pounds.

Sato was Goodluck's size but slender. You might think the man weak until you saw him fight. Trained in Japanese fighting, Sato was a man to be reckoned with if crossed.

They mounted up and rode the horses the one mile to the railroad depot to wait for the train.

Cavill lit one of his Cuban cigars. Goodluck stuffed and lit his pipe. They sat on a bench to wait for the train.

"When we catch Valdez, I'm going to beat him to death," Cavill said. "None of this trial crap where he might be sent back to Mexico, where he'll likely escape."

"We need him alive if we're to find all those children," Goodluck said. "Finding the children is the goal, not killing Valdez."

"Leave it to you to make sense," Cavill said.

Sato grinned. "If one of those children was yours, would you want him alive to talk?" he said.

"Bookends," Cavill said. "I'm working with bookends."

"Our job is to find Valdez and see what we can do about rescuing all these captured children," Goodluck said. "Not to seek revenge."

"One can be the other at the same time," Cavill said. "And you're sounding more like Jim every day."

"Train's coming," Goodluck said.

After the train arrived, they loaded the horses into the boxcar, boarded the train, and went to their sleeper cars to drop off their luggage.

"We'll meet in the dining car at eight-thirty," Cavill said.

In his car, Cavill tossed his suitcase in the corner of the room and tested the bed. He checked the wallet in his suit jacket pocket. He'd drawn two thousand dollars in expense money, but he'd also brought a few hundred of his own. There was nothing to do on a three-day train ride except play cards, and he planned on doing quite a bit of that.

In his car, Goodluck opened his luggage and fished out a book. It was *Twenty Thousand Leagues Under the Sea,* by Jules Verne. One habit Goodluck picked up as an army scout was reading. There was little to do after a day's ride when you stopped to make camp, and he noticed many of the soldiers passed the time reading books. What the soldiers called dime novels. He took to borrowing them and became hooked on reading. Whenever he could, he would buy what was new from general stores and bookshops.

He enjoyed Verne immensely, his tales of what they called science fiction. He disliked the fake dime novels that portrayed Billy the Kid and other outlaws as heroes when they were not.

Sato set his luggage on the bed and removed his jacket so he could wash his face in the washbasin.

He was most anxious to see his wife and children, but he wasn't sure how his wife would take his news about working for the agency instead of the railroad.

It wasn't a question of money. He had made quite a bit of it working for the railroad the past fifteen years. It wasn't a question of being home. His wife was used to him being away for weeks, sometimes months, on a job.

At this stage of his life, Sato was established and had job security for as long as he wanted it. He couldn't explain it even to himself, but he was bored doing what he was doing. Working with men like Cavill, Goodluck, and Duffy was exciting and gave him a sense of purpose that building bridges couldn't match.

He couldn't remember the last time he did something that excited him in such a way as riding with these men did.

Of course, no one shot at him or tried to kill him as a bridge designer, but that aside, he hoped his wife would understand.

At eight-thirty, Cavill, Goodluck, and Sato met in the dining car.

Cavill ordered six fried eggs, a half-pound of bacon, home fries, toast, and coffee.

Goodluck and Sato ordered pancakes.

As they ate, they discussed business.

"First thing we'll do in San Francisco is meet with the police department," Cavill said. "Map it out, see if there are any witnesses, and then wire Jim at the office. Quill and Harvey will likely be doing the same in Saint Louis."

"So many children," Sato said. "It seems an impossible task."

"If there's a chance for us to save even one kid, I'll wring that bastard's neck like he was a chicken to find out where those children are," Cavill said.

"First we need to find him," Goodluck said.

"It occurs to me that it isn't enough to simply abduct these children," Sato said. "There must be a market for them as well."

"Bookends," Cavill said as he ate an entire fried egg in one bite. "I'm working with bookends."

CHAPTER SEVEN

Quill and Harvey put their horses in the boxcar and then boarded the ten a.m. train bound for Saint Louis.

If the train ran on time, they would reach Saint Louis by four in the afternoon.

They went to the dining car and ordered coffee. Miss Potts had reserved a room for them at a hotel just a few blocks from police headquarters, so they could get a fresh start in the morning.

Both men were thirty-five and unmarried, although both had steady girlfriends.

They had been partners going on five years. They were experienced soldiers and police officers and were well versed in forensics, ballistics, and investigative work.

"It still seems like a dream the old man is gone," Quill said.

"We have to make sure he didn't die for nothing," Harvey said.

"There's far more to this than abducted

children and Porter's murder," Quill said. "There is an entire market out there for slave children. That's the really frightening part in all of this."

"Valdez and his people wouldn't be kidnapping these children if someone wasn't willing to pay good money for them," Harvey said.

"To those people, these kids are no different from the beans farmers grow to make this cup of coffee," Quill said. "If we didn't drink it, they wouldn't grow it."

"Slavery was abolished more than two decades ago in the US, never existed in Canada and Mexico, and even Cuba did away with slavery fifteen years ago, so where is the market?" Harvey said.

"Good question," Quill said.

"The Orient?" Harvey said.

"Could be," Quill said. "Could be anywhere."

Coffee finished, they went to a riding car and took seats beside a window. The scenery rolled by at fifty miles per hour.

"What's the advantage of kidnapping a rich child over a poor child if not for ransom?" Quill said.

"A child from a wealthy family eats better food, tends to be healthier and better dressed," Harvey said.

"And better educated," Quill said. "Whatever they're being sold for, an educated kid learns faster."

"The boys maybe," Harvey said. "I don't think they want the girls for their education."

"Good God," Quill said.

CHAPTER EIGHT

Duffy and Miss Potts boarded the east-bound train for Washington, D.C. at noon. If the train ran on time, they would reach D.C. at around six a.m. the following morning.

Both had eaten a large breakfast earlier, so they went directly to their sleeping cars and made plans to meet for dinner in the dining car at six p.m.

Miss Potts flagged a passing porter and asked for a pot of tea. When the tea was delivered, she poured a cup, sat at the small desk, and opened her briefcase.

Porter had made dozens of pages of notes, which she had typed, concerning Valdez and the missing children.

She looked at the artist's sketch of Valdez. He was a cruel-looking man in the sketch but even more so in person. Although she only saw Valdez from a distance and for just a few seconds, his face was permanently etched in her mind.

She hoped that when he was caught, he was alive so she could attend his hanging. She'd look into those cruel eyes and spit at him.

Miss Potts read all of Porter's reports on the case and then stuffed them back into the briefcase.

She was unaware she was crying until tears fell on a page.

"Oh damn," she said aloud.

Duffy removed the flask of whiskey from his luggage, poured an ounce into a water glass, and then filled the glass with water.

He lit one of Porter's Cuban cigars and sat in the chair at the small writing table.

His mind was crowded with thoughts. Thoughts of Valdez, of Kathy, of running the agency — a job he'd never wanted — of law school and his future.

Valdez wasn't just a murderer; he was a pirate. A pirate who dealt in stolen children as a commodity. Valdez was the seller, but who was the buyer?

How many buyers were there?

Close to two hundred and fifty children had disappeared to date. From San Francisco to New York. From Chicago to Saint Louis. Philadelphia to Dallas. No children had been reported missing from small towns or poor communities. Valdez's operation was a well-oiled machine.

He . . . Duffy paused and opened his briefcase and removed some documents. New York, San Francisco, Chicago, Saint Louis, and Philadelphia were all major port towns. Dallas to the Red River to Galveston; a major port town was just a few days on a riverboat.

The kids were being shanghaied, for God's sake.

San Francisco on the West Coast; New York, Philadelphia, Boston, and Galveston to the east.

Boys for galley mates and cheap labor on merchant ships.

Girls to the Far East for labor in the home and, when they got a bit older, for the master's amusement.

Duffy made pages of notes to bring to the Justice Department.

Mentally exhausted, he took a nap.

Duffy found Miss Potts at a table in the dining car when he entered a bit after six o'clock.

"If you don't mind me saying so, you look exhausted," Miss Potts said.

"This is one time I feel worse than I look,"

Duffy said.

"Let's have some dinner. You'll feel better," Miss Potts said.

They ordered baked chicken, and Duffy told Miss Potts his theory about the port cities.

"I'd say that's more than just a theory," Miss Potts said.

"What time do Quill and Harvey arrive in Saint Louis?" Duffy said.

"Four o'clock," Miss Potts said.

"The first order of business is to send them a telegram from a water stop," Duffy said.

CHAPTER NINE

Quill and Harvey went to dinner at their hotel's restaurant. The hotel was located one mile from police headquarters.

The hotel had its own stable, and they boarded their horses there. They noticed that street traffic was mostly horse-drawn carriages, so they might not need their horses for travel, taking horse-drawn taxis instead.

After dinner, they stopped at the desk to send a telegram to Duffy and found one waiting for them.

They took the telegram to a sofa in the lobby and read it.

After reading the contents, Quill said, "We best get our briefcases and meet in the bar. We have some work to do."

In the gaming car, Cavill was engaged in a marathon game of poker with five other men. He started the game with one hundred dollars, went down eighty, and then came back several hundred.

The gaming car had a waiter who supplied a steady round of bourbon. Cavill, feeling generous, supplied Cuban cigars to men who wanted one. The game started after dinner. At midnight, Cavill left the table up twenty dollars.

After dinner, Goodluck returned to his cabin and read his book for several hours. The story of Captain Nemo was complicated on many levels. Some of it was difficult to understand in the way *Moby Dick* had been when he'd read it several years ago.

He paused to fix a small drink of bourbon and water and stuff his pipe. He continued reading until there was a soft knock on the door.

"Yes?" Goodluck said.

"It's Sato. I was wondering if I could interest you in a game of chess," Sato said.

Goodluck opened the door. Sato had a chessboard and a small box under his arm along with a bottle of wine.

"I was getting tired of reading anyway," Goodluck said.

"Where is Mr. Cavill?" Sato said.

"Jack is either playing cards or fighting," Goodluck said. "Sometimes he does both at the same time."

Sato set up the game. The he took two thimble-sized cups from his pocket and filled each one with wine.

"Japanese wine called sake. Made from rice. It's very strong," Sato said.

Sato played white, Goodluck black. After several moves, Goodluck sampled the wine. It was, as Sato said, very strong.

After a dozen moves, Sato said, "There is something I've been studying."

Goodluck looked up from the board.

"San Francisco is a major port city with ships coming and going every day," Sato said. "So are New York, Chicago, Philadelphia, and Saint Louis. I believe that's why Valdez targeted these cities: for easy access to merchant ships. What I can't figure out is Dallas. It has no port."

"From Dallas to the Red River is a short trip," Goodluck said. "Downriver to Galveston takes just a few days. Galveston is a major port."

"We must discuss this with the San Francisco Police so they can watch the docks," Sato said.

"I agree, but Valdez has probably moved on by now," Goodluck said. "To San Diego or even Los Angeles. Maybe north to Portland or Seattle."

"We must telegraph Mr. Duffy in Washington about this," Sato said.

"Knowing Jim as I do, I expect he figured it out long before us," Goodluck said. He looked at the board. "It's your move."

CHAPTER TEN

Duffy and Miss Potts took a taxi from the railroad to the hotel about one mile from the White House.

Barely sunrise, the streets were grey and quiet. At the hotel, a porter took their bags and carried them to the front desk. After checking in, Duffy and Porter went to their rooms and made plans to meet at eight o'clock for breakfast.

Duffy washed up, shaved, and changed his suit.

Miss Potts washed up, fixed her hair, and changed her skirt and blouse.

They met in the dining hall and ordered a full breakfast of eggs, bacon, potatoes, toast, juice, and coffee.

"Our appointment at the Justice Department is at ten o'clock," Duffy said.

"I wish Mr. Porter could be here," Miss Potts said.

"He is, Miss Potts," Duffy said. "Believe

me, he is."

Quill and Harvey took a taxi from the hotel to police headquarters. The building was a three-story, white brick structure designed to withstand nothing short of a tornado.

Uniformed police officers were out front, coming and going.

The lobby was also crowded with uniformed officers that Quill and Harvey had to navigate around to reach the front desk. A sergeant manned the desk. Behind him, two telegraph operators were on duty.

"Can I help you gentlemen?" the sergeant said.

"We have an appointment with Captain Wakefield," Quill said.

The sergeant looked at the logbook on the desk. "I'll have an officer bring you up," he said.

Duffy and Miss Potts arrived at the Justice Department at ten a.m. and were escorted to the office of Federal Prosecutor Tom Poule. Poule was a short man in his fifties, who rose up the ranks through sheer determination and dedication to the law.

Fierce in a courtroom, he could not be bribed or dissuaded when prosecuting a case that reached the federal level.

"I've studied every document Mr. Porter and your agency sent me," Poule said. "And as you already know, you've been given authority to pursue Valdez and bring him to justice. No taking it upon yourself, no frontier justice, or I revoke your authority. Are we clear on that point, Mr. Duffy, Miss Potts?"

"We don't operate any other way," Duffy said.

"Good. That said, I am truly sorry about Charles Porter. He was a fine man and will be missed," Poule said.

"Mr. Poule, we have some new information we'd like you to look at," Duffy said.

"Let's move to the conference table," Poule said. "I'll send out for some coffee."

Captain Wakefield read all of Quill and Harvey's documents and sighed heavily. "I have one hundred uniformed police officers and six detectives to protect a city with a population of three hundred and fifty thousand souls. I am not surprised a man like Valdez can operate unfettered," he said.

"How many US Marshals are assigned to Saint Louis?" Quill said.

"Three," Wakefield said.

"The county sheriff's department?" Harvey said.

"Stays outside the city unless requested," Wakefield said.

"It's highly unlikely Valdez is still in Saint Louis, but have your printshop make enough copies for all your officers," Quill said.

"We'd like to see the parks where children were abducted and then the port," Harvey said.

"The port?" Wakefield said.

"Every city Valdez has struck in has access to a major port," Quill said. "He probably had a ship waiting and then sailed down the Mississippi to the ocean."

"Yes, of course," Wakefield said. "I'll assign two detectives to show you around."

Poule studied Duffy's maps, charts, and documents carefully. "I have to agree these children are being shanghaied using our ports of entry," he said. "This tells me Valdez's operation is highly organized and well financed."

"In order for Valdez to operate so freely, many hands have to be greased," Duffy said. "Can you have US Marshals confiscate shipping records from each of these ports and sent to your office?"

"I shall send out telegrams today," Poule said.

"We'll stay in Washington until they arrive," Duffy said.

"Mr. Duffy, Mr. Porter talked a great deal about you on his trips to Washington," Poule said. "If you get your law degree, you will make a fine federal prosecutor. Give it some thought."

"After Valdez is apprehended," Duffy said.

"Of course," Poule said.

Quill and Harvey, accompanied by two Saint Louis detectives, toured the two parks where nine children had vanished.

The parks were in the wealthiest neighborhoods of the city. Fashionably dressed mothers and nannies pushed strollers or held the hands of their children. Some sat on benches while children played.

The park was hilly, with sloping lawns and trees and many paths. Turn a corner, and a path disappeared. The second park was much the same.

Valdez was long gone by now, off to another city, or perhaps on one of the ships to deliver the children to their destination.

The question was: deliver them where?

"We'd like to see the port now," Quill told a detective.

Poule took Duffy and Miss Potts to lunch

at a fashionable restaurant on the hill. It was full of senators, congressmen, judges, and power brokers.

"We don't know where Valdez is from, but the Justice Department should be prepared for an international incident," Duffy said. "With whom or how many countries, we don't know at the moment, but you can bet it's more than one."

Poule nodded. "I'll speak to the attorney general and state department and advise them to talk to the president."

"Every major port city should be put on alert," Miss Potts said. "From Maine to Florida on the East Coast, and from Washington State to San Diego on the West Coast."

"Agreed," Poule said.

"Why is everybody staring at me?" Miss Potts said. "Haven't they ever seen a woman before?"

Poule grinned. "Not in here," he said.

The port was enormous, with docks and ships everywhere. Teamsters were loading and unloading cargo on nearly every ship.

"We need to see the harbormaster," a detective said.

The harbormaster glared at Quill and

Harvey after the detectives made their request.

"Do you have any idea how many ships have come and gone in the past month?" the harbormaster said. "A hundred or more. We get three coming and going every day, and sometimes more."

A detective reached into a pocket for an envelope. "This is a warrant signed by a judge," he said. "I can have twenty police officers here in an hour. They will take everything, and that includes that little box in your safe where you keep your graft money."

The harbormaster looked at Quill and Harvey. "What do you want to see?" he said.

Poule, Duffy, and Miss Potts stood over the conference table in Poule's office and studied a map of the United States.

Using a red pencil, Duffy highlighted the cities where children had been abducted and traced rivers and ports to the ocean.

"My God, man, we're talking about thousands of ships," Poule said.

"More, when you take into account the transfer ships moving goods from Saint Louis and Chicago and Dallas to ocean ports for transfer," Duffy said.

"How is it possible so many children can

be smuggled out of the country right under our noses?" Poule said.

"Money," Duffy said. "It buys a lot of silence."

Quill, Harvey, and the two detectives worked until well after dark in the harbormaster's office.

They divided the ships' manifests into four piles and then copied the information onto clean paper.

"Look, I have to get home to my wife and kids," the harbormaster said. "Maybe if you told me what you're looking for, I could help?"

"You just be quiet until we're done," a detective said.

Once the manifests were copied, Quill, Harvey, and the detectives took a taxi to police headquarters.

"You men must be hungry," Quill said. "Why not join us for dinner at our hotel as our guests."

At the hotel dining room, Miss Potts cut into her steak and said, "I think I'll return home tomorrow."

"I need you here," Duffy said.

"Someone has to run the office," Miss Potts said. "There are six other agents sitting around twiddling their thumbs while the work piles up. I can be of more use back home."

Duffy nodded. "Agreed," he said.

"You'll see me off in the morning?" Miss Potts said.

"Of course," Duffy said.

Quill, Harvey, and the two detectives had a late dinner at the hotel.

"So what now?" a detective said.

"We'll return to the office, contact our supervisor, and proceed from there," Quill said.

"Valdez won't return to Saint Louis, will he?" the other detective said.

"Not likely. If he does, it won't be for some time," Harvey said.

"Even so, we should keep the city on alert," a detective said.

"Yes, even so," Quill said.

CHAPTER ELEVEN

Whenever he was really bored, Cavill would find someone to fight or would work out on the makeshift heavy bag he rigged in the yard behind his house.

Without either at his disposal, Cavil removed his shirt and did push-ups and sit-ups on the floor of his riding car. Hundreds of each until his chest, arms, and shoulders burned, and his lungs were on fire.

Only when he was too exhausted to do one more push-up did he finally quit.

By tomorrow morning they would be in San Francisco, but right now he faced another eighteen hours of nothing to do.

There wasn't even a decent card player on the whole stinking train to pass the time with.

When he finally got off the floor, Cavill filled the washbasin, sponged off the sweat, then shaved.

Refreshed, he dressed and left the car to

find Goodluck and Sato.

They were in the gentlemen's car, playing chess.

Cavill went to the bar, ordered a glass of bourbon, took it to the table where Goodluck and Sato were playing chess, and took a seat. He removed a Cuban cigar from his boot and lit it with a match.

Goodluck puffed on his pipe.

"Who's winning?" Cavill said.

"That's not how chess is played," Goodluck said.

"I have to get off this train," Cavill said. "One more night on this stupid train and I'm gonna bust a gut."

Sato slid his bishop across the board and captured Goodluck's pawn.

"Well, that was exciting," Cavill said.

Across the room, six men were engaged in a card game. One man, slightly drunk, suddenly stood up and walked to the bar. "Whiskey," he said to the bartender.

"I think you've had enough, sir," the bartender said.

"I'll say when I've had enough," the man said.

The bartender filled a glass with whiskey and the man gulped half of it down in one swallow. "Look at this, barkeep," he said. "They let anybody on a train these days."

Cavill looked at the man.

"We got us a redskin savage and a Chinaman," the man said. "Next thing you know, they'll expect us to ride with coloreds."

Cavill stood up and walked to the bar and looked at the man. "You shut your mouth," he said.

"Why?" the man said. "It's a free country, isn't it? Free speech and all that bullshit. I can say whatever I please."

"Say it somewhere else," Cavill said.

The man looked up at Cavill, at the sheer size of the man, and nodded.

"Goodbye," Cavill said.

The man turned as if to walk away, then reached into his jacket for a derringer. Before he could cock the hammer, Cavill punched him in the jaw with a right hook that sent him unconscious to the floor.

"You're right about one thing, mister. They let anybody ride the trains these days," Cavill said.

Goodluck, studying the board, never looked up.

"Did you see that?" Sato said.

"A thousand times before," Goodluck said.

Cavill returned to his chair. "Let's get something to eat," he said.

■ ■ ■ ■

Duffy was in Poule's office after lunch, studying the maps and charts, when an aide delivered a telegram.

"For Mr. Duffy," the aide said.

Duffy read the telegram. "Our men in Saint Louis got copies of the ships' manifests for the previous month," he told Poule.

"Have them sent here," Poule said. "You'll stay on until we hear from the marshals and your people in San Francisco."

"Wait for a reply," Duffy told the aide.

"Tell me about your John L. Sullivan," Sato said as he sliced into his baked chicken.

Eating a steak, Cavill said, "He's the heavyweight champion boxer of the world."

"And you wish to fight him?" Sato said.

"I can beat him," Cavill said.

"How do you know until you fight the man?" Sato said.

"You feel it," Cavill said and tapped his chest. "In here."

"I've seen Sullivan fight," Goodluck said. "Jack can beat him."

"Hopefully someday you will get that opportunity," Sato said.

"If we ever get off this stinking train,"

Cavill said.

By the end of the day, Duffy and Poule were tired and bleary eyed from reading reports and making notes. They wanted dinner and an early night.

The early night was not forthcoming.

An aide knocked on Poule's door.

"The president wants to see you," the aide said. "Both of you."

"Right now?" Poule said.

"Right now," the aide said.

CHAPTER TWELVE

President Chester Arthur was Duffy's height, a bit overweight, and had a great set of mutton-chop sideburns.

He received Poule and Duffy in the Oval Office.

"I realize it's late in the day, but I am greatly concerned about this Valdez business," Arthur said. "I understand that you and your agency are heading up this investigation along with Mr. Poule here."

"Yes sir," Duffy said.

"My God, man, this has the capability of being an international incident," Arthur said.

"I doubt that Valdez is operating with permission of any foreign government," Duffy said.

"That may be true, but any foreign government involved will have to agree to co-operate in order to bring those children home," Arthur said. "To take them by force would be an act of war."

"Understood," Poule said.

"The United States is second behind Great Britain in world power at the moment," Arthur said. "By 1900 we will have eclipsed them. The last thing we want is to appear to be a bloodthirsty nation of savages. The Civil War is just twenty years behind us, and we must not let our guard down for one moment when it comes to foreign policy. Understood?"

"Yes sir," Poule said.

"Mr. Duffy?" Arthur said.

"Perfectly clear, sir."

"That said, I want Valdez found and brought to Washington for trial," Arthur said. "You use any and all means to find the son of a bitch, no matter what it costs. And Goddammit, we need to get those children back home where they belong."

Duffy and Poule had a late dinner at Duffy's hotel.

"Are you a married man, Jim?" Poule said.

"No," Duffy said. "Not at the moment."

"Good," Poule said. "A wife deserves a husband who is home more than he's not. In this business, wives tend to get lost in the shuffle."

"Mr. Porter had a policy of not hiring

married men," Duffy said. "Partly because of the long hours and days away from home, but also because he didn't want to create any widows."

"Sounds like a good policy," Poule said.

Duffy nodded. "President Arthur is right about an international incident," he said.

"I know," Poule said.

"The only person who knows where these children are being sold is Valdez," Duffy said. "Our priority is to capture him alive, or we'll never get them back."

"He won't talk for free," Poule said. "He'll want a deal, and a sweet one at that."

"Give it to him," Duffy said. "And then ship him back to wherever he came from for punishment."

"That may be the only way," Poule said.

"In the morning, can you send a telegram to the Mexican Federal Police and ask them if they know of a King Valdez?" Duffy said.

Poule looked at Duffy. "I can do that," he said.

Chapter Thirteen

San Francisco was home to a quarter-million residents, and it seemed as if every one of them was in the streets at the same time.

"This place is a mess," Cavill said as he, Goodluck, and Sato walked their horses from the railroad station through town.

Horse-drawn carriages clogged the streets. Uniformed police officers stood in the middle of the street, directing traffic. Telegraph lines were everywhere.

"Let's find our hotel first and then get some breakfast," Cavill said.

They had reserved two rooms at the Continental. Sato would stay with his wife and family at their rented residence.

Sato parted ways with Cavill and Goodluck with plans to meet at the hotel later in the afternoon.

"Every time I come to this town, it seems like I get more and more lost," Cavill said.

"Let's ask one of these policemen."

After getting directions to their hotel, they walked ten blocks to the hotel and checked in. The hotel had a small livery for the horses.

"Do you have a telegraph line?" Cavill said to the desk clerk.

"Of course," the clerk said.

"I need to send a wire," Cavill said.

The clerk gave Cavill paper and pencil. "We'll add the telegram to your bill," he said.

Sato's wife, Yuki, hugged him so tightly he could barely breathe.

"I thought you'd never come home," she said in Japanese.

"English, please," Sato said. "We are in America."

"Yes, of course," Yuki said in English.

"Where are the girls?" Sato said.

"At school," Yuki said. "I will pick them up at three."

"Good, then we have time to talk," Sato said. "We have much to discuss."

"What should we do first?" Goodluck said when he met Cavill in the lobby.

"Take a walk around town," Cavill said. "We don't meet with the police chief until tomorrow morning, so we might as well get familiarized."

"Let's ask the desk clerk," Goodluck said.

The clerk gave them a walking tour map of the downtown section of San Francisco. Highlights included Chinatown, the wharf, the bay, and several major parks. An entire section was for shopping.

Cavill and Goodluck walked the streets, taking in the sights, until Cavill saw the banner strung across Union Square.

Heavyweight Champion John L. Sullivan Exhibition Fight Tomorrow At The Union Square Hotel.

Cavill stared at the banner.

"Jack, we're on assignment," Goodluck said.

"I know, I know, but we have nothing to do anyway," Cavill said.

"Jack, we . . ." Goodluck said as Cavill took off.

"I don't understand," Yuki said. "What do you mean you want to give up being an engineer to become a . . . what did you call it?"

"Detective, and I didn't say permanently," Sato said. "This is something I feel compelled to do."

"But why?" Yuki said.

63

"If our two daughters were kidnapped, when would you expect me to stop looking for them?" Sato said.

Yuki stared at Sato.

"What shall we serve for dinner tonight?" Sato said. "Jack Cavill eats enough for three men."

In the grand ballroom of the Union Square Hotel, a boxing ring had been assembled and, in the ring, John L. Sullivan was skipping rope. A dozen newspaper reporters sat in chairs and made notes.

A crowd of a hundred was gathered around the ring.

A man stepped into the ring. "Attention everybody," he said. "John needs a few sparring partners to work up a sweat. Ten dollars to any man willing to spar for one round. Any takers?"

Goodluck looked at Cavill. "Jack, don't," he said.

Cavill held up his right hand. "I'll do it," he said.

Ten minutes later, shirtless, Cavill stood in the ring opposite Sullivan. Sullivan stood seven inches shorter than Cavill, weighed two hundred and twelve pounds, and had fists like cannonballs.

"Nice and easy now, boys," the referee

said. "This is a sparring match, not the real thing."

"Sure, Boyle, no worries," Sullivan said. He looked at Cavill. "Where are you from, lad?"

"Chicago."

"I hail from Boston," Sullivan said.

"I know," Cavill said.

"Time," the referee said.

Sullivan and Cavill started out by slowly circling each other. Sullivan tossed a weak jab. Cavill hit Sullivan with a weaker straight right.

"You've got good balance, Boyle," Sullivan said and hit Cavill with a solid left hook to the jaw.

Cavill countered with an equally solid right cross to Sullivan's jaw, causing Sullivan to blink.

Sullivan stepped back and looked at Cavill. "Come on then, lad," he said.

"Yes," Cavill said.

For the next two minutes, Sullivan and Cavill tore into each other, pounding away with thunderous right hooks, jabs, left hooks, and combinations that had the spectators cheering.

"Time," the referee said and stepped between the two men.

Cavill had a welt under his left eye and

blood on his lips, but so did Sullivan.

"You're a professional, aren't you?" Sullivan said.

"One day we'll do this for real," Cavill said.

"Look forward to it," Sullivan said.

After Cavill washed up and dressed, he met Goodluck in the hotel lobby.

"I can beat that man, Joseph," Cavill said.

"I know," Goodluck said. "Can we get back to business now?"

"Damn," Cavill said.

"What?"

"I forgot my ten dollars," Cavill said.

Cavill and Goodluck found Sato waiting for them in the lobby of their hotel.

"You're invited to supper at my house," Sato said. "Jack, what happened to your face?"

"I'll tell you about it on the way," Cavill said. "What are we having? I'm starving."

Goodluck patted Sato on the back. "I hope your wife made enough to feed the 3rd Cavalry," he said.

CHAPTER FOURTEEN

The office was a mess. Upon arriving in the early afternoon, Miss Potts organized unanswered telegrams, sorted the mail, and swept all the floors.

She was surprised when Quill and Harvey walked into the office around three o'clock.

"We thought you were in Washington," Quill said.

"And I thought you were in Saint Louis," Miss Potts said.

"We finished up and sent our reports to Jim," Harvey said.

"We recorded the manifest of over a hundred ships," Quill said.

"Do you have copies for the office?" Miss Potts said.

"We do," Harvey said.

"Let's have a look," Miss Potts said.

"Had lunch?" Quill said.

"I haven't," Miss Potts said.

"Our treat," Quill said.

Miss Potts read the reports as she, Quill, and Harvey ate a late lunch at a restaurant near the office.

"The children could have been shanghaied onto any number of these ships," she said.

"We know," Quill said.

"And taken anywhere in the world," Miss Potts said.

"We were talking about that on the train," Quill said.

"How much do you think a healthy, educated child will sell for on the black market?" Harvey said. "Five thousand dollars? Ten? Twenty? More?"

"If you look at the sheer number of missing children, it's a multimillion-dollar business," Quill said.

"Those doing the buying need to be wealthy in their own right," Harvey said.

"Boys to work on plantations and in mines," Harvey said. "Girls for . . . well, we know what for."

"Good heavens," Miss Potts said.

"When we get back to the office, we figured to do some additional work on the reports," Quill said. "Maybe we missed something."

■ ■ ■ ■

Back at the office, Quill, Harvey, and Miss Potts studied the list of ship manifests and started separate lists.

By cargo.

Name.

By destination.

By how many visits to port.

Cargo was everything from hardware to lumber to home furnishings to ladies' dresses and skirts.

Destinations were the Mississippi Delta in the Gulf of Mexico.

"For loading onto seaworthy ships for delivery," Miss Potts said.

"This ship was recorded three times in Port Saint Louis," Quill said. "The *Elizabeth*. Cargo listed as home goods. Destination: Mississippi Delta."

"Where is it registered?" Harvey said.

"It isn't," Quill said. "It's a privateer."

"How long will it take you to get to the Mississippi Delta?" Miss Potts said.

"If we left in the morning, about twenty hours," Quill said.

Miss Potts went to the safe and removed the cashbox.

"Go book your tickets," she said. "I'll send

a wire to Jim."

"Will you tell him why?" Quill said.

"He'll have figured it out by now," Miss Potts said.

CHAPTER FIFTEEN

Minus their shoes, Cavill and Goodluck followed Sato into the living room where his family waited.

"Joseph Goodluck, Jack Cavill, my wife, Yuki, and my daughters, Yumi and Yui," Sato said.

"Very pleased to meet you, ma'am," Cavill said.

"Same here," Goodluck said.

"You're big," Yui said.

"Do you know what he eats to get so big?" Sato said to Yui. "Thirteen-year-old girls with noodles."

Yumi spoke to Yuki in Japanese. Yuki smiled. "She wants to know what he eats for dessert," Yuki said.

Yuki prepared an American dinner of steaks, potatoes, carrots, and corn and served cold lemonade to drink.

For dessert she made *suama,* a Japanese dessert made from rice, flour, sugar, and red food coloring.

"This is wonderful," Cavill said.

"Please take more," Yuki said. "Don't be shy."

"Jack is many things, but shy isn't one of them," Goodluck said.

"Are you a real Indian?" Yui said to Goodluck.

"I am," Goodluck said.

"We don't see Indians in San Francisco," Yui said.

"Girls, that's enough talk," Sato said. "Mr. Cavill, Mr. Goodluck, and I have much to discuss."

"Do you prefer coffee or tea?" Yuki said.

"Coffee," Sato said. "We will be in the study."

Sato poured coffee and said, "Please feel free to smoke."

Cavill lit a cigar and Goodluck smoked his pipe.

"In the morning we must meet with the police chief of San Francisco," Sato said.

"And after that the harbormaster," Cavill said.

"Maybe there will be a reply from Jim when we get back to the hotel," Goodluck said.

"I want to see the park where the kids disappeared," Cavill said.

"I shall meet you at the hotel at nine o'clock tomorrow morning," Sato said.

Cavill stopped at the hotel desk. A telegram from Duffy was waiting for them.

"Let's have a nightcap and see what Jim has to say," Cavill said.

Cavill brought two small glasses of whiskey to a sofa where Goodluck waited.

"Open it, let's see what's on Jim's mind," Cavill said.

Goodluck opened the sealed envelope, read it quickly, then passed it to Cavill.

"About what we were going to do anyway," Cavill said.

"A privateer ship is?" Goodluck said.

"A ship that operates alone as a private enterprise," Cavill said. "It hires out to anybody that pays for its service."

"Such as smuggling children," Goodluck said.

"Yeah," Cavill said. "Like smuggling children."

CHAPTER SIXTEEN

Miss Potts arrived at the office a bit before nine o'clock. She had a light breakfast at home of one egg, two slices of toast with butter, and coffee.

In the office, she fired up the woodstove in the break room and made a pot of coffee. While the coffee boiled, a telegram arrived by messenger. It was from Duffy.

Miss Potts read the telegram as she drank a cup of coffee. Duffy wanted the Port of Chicago checked for ships' manifests, with particular attention paid to privateer ships. He recommended Quill and Harvey go to Chicago.

By now, Quill and Harvey were on a train to Mississippi.

Miss Potts searched the availability of other agents not on assignment. Lester Holt had recently returned from the field and should be at home.

Lester Holt was the oldest agent employed

by the agency. He was forty-five, an attorney, and had been hired by Porter to interpret the legality of certain circumstances where the political water was muddy, so to speak.

Holt still had his private practice, although his client list was limited. He made a great deal of money, so he was no longer motivated by it and worked only on cases that interested him.

Miss Potts left the office, went to the company stables, and hitched up the buggy. The ride to Holt's home took about twenty minutes.

Holt lived in a two-story home on a back street. A nice lawn and garden were out front. Miss Potts parked the buggy, went to the door, and knocked.

"Miss Potts, what a surprise," Holt said. "Come in for some coffee."

"No time, Lester," Miss Potts said. "We have to go to Chicago right away."

"Chicago? What for?"

"I'll explain on the way," Miss Potts said.

In the dining car on the train, Miss Potts and Holt ate lunch while Holt read the reports about the missing children.

"Charles was onto something here," Holt said.

"Here is a copy of authorization from the Justice Department," Miss Potts said and produced the document from her handbag.

Holt scanned the document. "Yes, we'll need this," he said.

"We arrive in Chicago at four o'clock," Miss Potts said. "We have a solid contact in Detective Sergeant Willis. We'll see him first."

"Unless I'm mistaken, the Illinois River flows to the Mississippi to the Gulf of Mexico," Holt said.

"Quill and Harvey are on the way to the Gulf right now," Miss Potts said. "They should arrive sometime before dawn."

Miss Potts hated Chicago, with its foul smelling streets, tall buildings, and over-crowded population. Sections of the city were exclusive, reserved for the wealthy elite. Other sections were dirt poor and filthy.

Rich or poor, the air smelled of coal and horse manure.

Miss Potts and Holt each took one bag with them. They loaded them onto a taxi and instructed the driver to take them to police headquarters.

They arrived at the large brick building at twenty minutes before five. By the time they spoke to the appropriate people, Detective Sergeant Willis, who had worked with the Agency before, met them in the lobby at five o'clock.

"Miss Potts, what are you doing in Chicago?" Willis said.

"We need to talk," Miss Potts said.

"Come to my office," Willis said.

By seven o'clock, Willis had read all the documents and discussed the matter of the missing children with the chief of police.

Then he returned to his office where Miss Potts and Holt waited.

"Where are you staying?" Willis said.

"The Carlton," Miss Potts said.

"I'll pick you up at eight a.m. tomorrow morning by carriage, and we'll ride to the docks together," Willis said.

Chapter Seventeen

Cavill, Goodluck, and Sato spent the morning with the chief of police in his office. The chief read every document carefully and said, "This is most disturbing indeed."

"We need access to the waterfront," Cavill said. "To review the ships' manifests."

"I'll assign two detectives to take you to the docks in the morning," the chief said. "But be warned, these longshoremen are a tight-knit bunch and don't take to outsiders."

"They're not stupid enough to defy the Justice Department," Cavill said.

"Have you heard of Charles Darwin?" the chief said.

"Maybe," Cavill said.

"I read his book," Goodluck said.

"As have I," Sato said.

"What does this Darwin fellow have to do with anything?" Cavill said.

"Some of these longshoremen probably

came from apes," the chief said.

"We'd like to see the parks where the children were abducted," Sato said.

"I'll have two detectives take you," the chief said.

The detectives took Cavill, Goodluck, and Sato to Huntington Park in the exclusive Nob Hill section of the city. The park was an entire square city block. Hardly anybody was in the park, and there were certainly no women and children.

"The parks have been empty since the newspapers printed the story about the missing children," a detective said.

The park was accessible from nearly a dozen places and four streets.

"The problem with these snobby rich is they never think anything bad can happen to them," Cavill said. "They found out differently."

"The second park is an hour away by carriage," a detective said. "Maybe we should get lunch first."

They ate at a fashionable restaurant a few blocks from Huntington Park and then rode across town to Pacific Heights.

Established a decade earlier, Pacific Heights was an upscale neighborhood with a beautiful view of the ocean.

"What's that island out there?" Goodluck said.

"Fort Alcatraz," a detective said. "It was used as a military prison during the Civil War, and it is still used for military prisoners today."

The park was situated in the middle of the neighborhood with access from eight different openings.

As with Huntington Park, it was empty.

"Too little, too late," Cavill said. "Six kids disappeared from this park."

"According to your police reports, not one mother or nanny identified Valdez by the sketch," Goodluck said.

"By the time we received the reports and distributed them, it was too late," a detective said.

"Take us to the docks," Sato said.

"It's kind of late in the day to start an investigation," a detective said.

"But not too late to time how long it takes to go from here to there," Sato said.

From the park to the docks took fifty minutes, traveling at a moderate speed.

"He could have had those kids aboard a ship before anyone even knew they were gone," Cavill said.

"What time do the docks open in the morning?" Sato said.

"Seven," a detective said.

"Pick us up at the hotel at eight," Cavill said.

After dropping Cavill and Goodluck off at the hotel, the carriage took Sato to his home.

"Let's grab a shave and a bath before dinner," Cavill said.

"Good idea," Goodluck said.

Cleaned, refreshed, and wearing fresh clothes, Cavill and Goodluck met in the hotel restaurant.

The waiter recommended the baked chicken.

"They must get a hundred ships a month in San Francisco," Cavill said. "Probably more. I think Jim is right when he said to focus on the privateer ships."

"The Coast Guard should have been notified," Goodluck said. "That's what they do, isn't? Protect the coast against pirates and smuggling?"

"Without cause, the Coast Guard isn't going to stop a ship, especially from a major port," Cavill said.

"Valdez isn't going to stop because he's afraid of the Coast Guard," Goodluck said. "He'll smuggle the children into Mexico and use their ports."

"We should send a wire to Jim about that," Cavill said. "Right after dessert."

CHAPTER EIGHTEEN

Duffy and Poule returned from a late supper to Poule's office to work an even later night.

Poule's office had a small woodstove and he made a pot of coffee.

The conference table was littered with documents and notebooks. Poule filled two mugs with coffee and brought them to the table where Duffy was already seated.

"We have Saint Louis, Dallas, and Philadelphia manifests," Duffy said. "The smuggling vessels have to be the privateers."

"Valdez has to know, after killing Charles Porter, that we are onto his game," Poule said.

"Oh, he knows," Duffy said.

"The question is, what is he going to do about it?" Poule said.

"No legitimate shipping line is going to risk the penalty involved for smuggling children," Duffy said. "He has to know they would be scrutinized by the Coast Guard going forward."

"He either stops, or . . ." Poule said.

"Smuggles the kids into Mexico and uses their ports," Duffy said.

"I think you're right," Poule said. "I think that's exactly what Valdez will do."

"Who do you know in the Mexican judicial system?" Duffy said.

Poule nodded. "I'll send a wire in the morning," he said.

Duffy looked at the fresh stack of papers on the table. "We had a delivery while we went to dinner," he said.

On top of the pile was an unopened telegram. Duffy picked it up, opened the envelope, and removed the telegram.

"It's from Jack in San Francisco," he said. "He says Valdez will use Mexico to smuggle children going forward. They will tackle the port in the morning."

There was another telegram from Quill and Harvey. They were in Mississippi.

A third telegram was from Miss Potts. She and Lester Holt were in Chicago to check the port for privateer ships.

"Chicago to Mississippi using the Mississippi River," Duffy said.

"At least a dozen cities and towns could do likewise," Poule said.

84

"Say you were Valdez and making hundreds of thousands of dollars smuggling children; would you stop because the risk got higher?" Duffy said.

"No. I'd find another way," Poule said. "And the only other way would be south into Mexico."

"That telegram you're going to send to the Mexican judicial system, make it a good one," Duffy said. "We're going to need all the help we can get."

Poule picked up a thick, sealed telegram envelope, tore it open, and removed the contents. It was from the Mexican Federal Police in reply to the inquiry concerning King Valdez.

"King Valdez, age forty-five," Poule said. "Six feet tall, dark hair and eyes and has a scar the length of his right cheek from a knife fight at the age of seventeen. Spent ten years in federal prison for arson. Disappeared at the age of thirty. Assumed migrated to the United States. No known address in Mexico. No known family."

"That isn't much," Duffy said.

"If he's been living in the US for fifteen years, maybe he has a prison record here," Poule said. "Under Valdez or an alias."

"We know he used his real name to recruit associates," Duffy said. "But he could have a wife, kids, and a little house with a picket fence somewhere, for all we know."

"Jim, I'm very tired," Poule said. "Can we pick this up in the morning?"

"I could use some sleep myself," Duffy said.

In his hotel room, an exhausted Duffy tried and failed to fall asleep.

His thoughts turned to Kathy. She was in Fort Jones by now and hopefully packing to return to Springfield.

Hopefully, because he had no way of knowing if she was having second thoughts. She was a doctor, and the people in Fort Jones and the surrounding countryside needed her. She was all they had in the way of medical care.

In Springfield and Chicago, she was just another doctor.

If she returned to Springfield before he did, she would send a telegram.

If he returned to Springfield and she wasn't there, he would know she wasn't coming back.

CHAPTER NINETEEN

Miss Potts and Holt had breakfast at seven a.m. in the hotel restaurant. Detective Sergeant Willis arrived promptly at eight o'clock to take them to the docks.

They arrived just before nine.

The docks were a frenzy of activity. Cargo ships were being loaded and unloaded. Dock workers and teamsters were everywhere, and the activity was conducted at a feverish pace.

Detective Willis, Miss Potts, and Holt found the harbormaster in his office behind his desk.

After showing his credentials, Willis stated the nature of the visit.

"Are you daft, man?" the harbormaster said. "This is Chicago, not some riverbed crossing in Missouri."

Willis produced a document from his jacket. "This is a warrant signed by a judge," he said. "Either you comply, or twenty uniformed officers will arrive within the hour, and they will tear this place apart. Whatever we find is ours, including that hidden cashbox filled with your bribe money."

"What do you want to see?" the harbormaster said.

"This is the port of San Francisco, man," the harbormaster said. "We are far too busy to waste time with your silly nonsense."

"We have a warrant," one of the two detectives said.

"You can wipe your Irish ass with that," the harbormaster said. "And then you can take this ugly Irish goon, his pet Chink, and your cigar-store Indian and get the hell out of my office."

Cavill stared at the harbormaster, who was seated behind his desk.

"Step back," Goodluck said.

"Why?" Sato said.

Goodluck yanked Sato out of the way a second before Cavill rushed forward, grabbed the harbormaster by the shirt, and hurled him over the desk to the floor.

"Oh," Sato said.

Cavill grabbed the harbormaster and lifted him to his feet. The harbormaster had a revolver shoved in the waistband of his pants and he reached for it. Cavill swatted it away and then wrapped his arms around the harbormaster and squeezed him.

Tight.

"Help . . . me," the harbormaster cried.

"We better stop this," a detective said.

"Be my guest," Goodluck said.

Cavill squeezed harder until the harbormaster surrendered. "Take whatever you want," he gasped.

Cavill opened his arms, and the harbormaster fell to the floor.

Quill and Harvey, along with two United States Marshals assigned to Mississippi, entered the harbormaster's office.

"What is going on here?" the harbormaster said.

"We're serving a federal warrant," a marshal said.

"For what?" the harbormaster said.

"Access to you ships' manifests," Quill said.

"Whatever for?" the harbormaster said.

"Ask the superior court judge who signed the warrant," Quill said.

"Get every ship manifest for the past thirty days," Harvey said.

"Every . . . That will take hours," the harbormaster said.

"Then you better get started," Quill said.

Sipping coffee in Poule's office, Duffy read the lengthy telegram Poule wrote to the Justice Department in Mexico at the capital of Mexico City.

Poule requested the Mexican Army patrol the border for Valdez and, if they captured him, to hold him for extradition to Washington.

"Two thousand miles of border," Duffy said. "From California to Texas. Trying to apprehend Valdez would be like trying to find one grain of sand on a beach."

"I can request US Marshals and the army keep an eye on the border," Poule said. "And the Texas Rangers."

"Good idea," Duffy said.

"I'll send this telegram," Poule said. "Then we can get some lunch."

After more than a week in Fort Jones, Kathy still hadn't packed a thing. The few weeks away from her practice had created a backlog of patients she still hadn't caught up on.

Broken legs and arms, bullet wounds, appendicitis, pneumonia, colic, and a host of other ailments had her working before dawn and into the night.

After a long, tiresome day, Kathy sat in

her parlor with a cup of tea.

She tried to relax, but her mind was filled with questions. She loved Jim, of that there was no doubt, but . . . was she needed in Springfield or Chicago?

By Jim, maybe.

By the medical profession, probably not. She would be just one more doctor in a sea of doctors and make little to no difference in the community.

She loved Jim and didn't want to give him up.

She became a doctor to make a difference, and she'd taken an oath to do so. In Fort Jones, she did.

There was a big decision to make.

A wagon stopped right outside her window. Loud footsteps came to the door.

"Doc Bodine, come quick," a voice cried out. "It's my wife."

Kathy went to the front door and opened it.

"Doc Bodine, my wife is powerful sick," the man said.

"I'll get my bag," Kathy said.

And without realizing it, the decision was made for her.

Josephine "Joey" Jordan sat on the front porch of her ranch house after a trip to

Helena and read the telegram from Cavill.

He was working on a really large and important case and traveling to San Francisco.

"San Francisco," Joey said aloud.

He missed her and wanted to see her, but this case was going to take some time and he didn't know when he would be back.

Joey sat and had a good cry. Then she went inside to the writing desk to write a letter to Cavill, telling him she was ending their relationship.

CHAPTER TWENTY

Miss Potts, Holt, and Detective Willis worked through the afternoon and broke for dinner at six o'clock.

They returned to the harbormaster's office at seven-thirty and finished up by ten o'clock. Afterward they rode back to the hotel and had a drink at the bar.

They had made a detailed record of every ship that came and went, including registration, cargo, and destination, going back thirty days.

Three privateer ships had stopped and taken on cargo before leaving for the Gulf of Mexico in Mississippi.

"I'll send a wire to Jim and ask him where he wants this information sent," Miss Potts said.

"It's been a long and tiring day," Willis said. "I'm going home to get some sleep. Stop by the office in the morning."

"Goodnight, Sergeant," Miss Potts said.

After Willis left the bar, Miss Potts and Holt had another drink before retiring to their rooms.

"Miss Potts, this has been a very stressful time," Holt said. "Losing Charles Porter, and now this Valdez business. I suggest after we wire Jim in the morning, we take the day to relax for a few hours. See some of the sights in Chicago before returning to Springfield."

Miss Potts nodded. "I guess we could use some relaxation at that, Lester," she said.

Sato and Goodluck waited on a sofa in the lobby of the hotel while Cavill sent a telegram to Duffy.

They spent ten hours at the harbormaster's office, where they compiled a very long and detailed list of cargo ships.

Seven privateer ships had picked up cargo in San Francisco. Any one of them could have transported those children.

Cavill entered the lobby. Goodluck and Sato stood up from the sofa.

"Let's get something to eat," Cavill said.

They entered the nearly empty restaurant and took a large table.

"Bring us a whiskey first," Cavill said.

The waiter left and returned a minute later with three shot glasses of whiskey.

"Care to bet those kids disappeared on a privateer ship," Cavill said.

"I've been thinking about Valdez," Sato said. "He has to know that all the ports he's operated out of are now being watched. He will have to stop his activity, find new ports, or move his operation south to Mexico. Correct?"

"That stands to reason," Cavill said. "The problem is, we don't know what he's going to do next or when."

"My point is, what if he does nothing?" Sato said. "He just quits while he's ahead."

"Then we have to root him out from where he is hiding," Cavill said.

"That could take years," Sato said. "Not to mention the manpower involved."

"If the ports are closed to him and the Mexican government is after him as well, he could do one of two things," Goodluck said. "Leave the country on one of his privateer ships or go north."

"Canada," Cavill said.

"It's a big country to hide out in," Goodluck said. "And not much different than the northern states."

"After we eat, I'll send another telegram to Jim about Canada," Cavill said.

"After we eat, I must go home," Sato said.

■ ■ ■ ■

After a long, exhausting day at the harbor-master's office, Quill and Harvey returned to their hotel and had a late supper.

They had copies of over one hundred ship manifests, of which ten were privateer ships.

Those ten ships were bound for Europe, the Far East, and South America.

The children could be anywhere in the world by now.

"I sent a telegram to Jim," Quill said. "See what he wants us to do next."

Asleep on the sofa in Poule's office, Duffy woke up when Poule said, "Jim, we just got one more telegram from your people."

Duffy opened his eyes and sat up.

"What time is it?" he said.

"Just after midnight," Poule said.

"The last telegram is from?" Duffy said.

"Agents Quill and Harvey in Mississippi," Poule said. "They are mailing their report on the ships."

"It will take two days for Quill and Harvey, another two for Miss Potts, and at least five for San Francisco," Duffy said.

"There is nothing more we can do to-night," Poule said. "I'm going home and sleep until ten. I suggest you do the same."

Duffy stood up and stretched his back. "Right," he said.

Chapter Twenty-One

Cavill and Goodluck arrived at Sato's home by taxi shortly before eight in the morning.

Sato greeted them at the door. "Please come in and have breakfast with my family."

Cavill and Goodluck removed their shoes and followed Sato to the dining room.

Yuki, Yumi, and Yui stood at the table.

"My wife has prepared a traditional American breakfast of steak and eggs," Sato said.

"I hope you like it," Yuki said.

"Please sit," Sato said. "You must be hungry."

Miss Potts and Holt had breakfast at the hotel and then looked at a tour book in the lobby.

"I would like to see the museum of natural history and the art museum," Miss Potts said.

"That won't take all day," Holt said.

"Maybe we can see the lake afterward."

"I would like that," Miss Potts said.

They took a taxi to the museum of natural history and spent several hours touring exhibits. At eleven o'clock, they walked the few blocks to the art museum.

At one o'clock, they had lunch at a small, outdoor café.

"Chicago is a fine city," Holt said.

"It is, but there are too many people for me," Miss Potts said. "And the air downtown is most foul."

"Jim should have sent a telegram to the hotel by now," Holt said. "I expect he'll want us back at the office."

"We can be on the ten o'clock train in the morning," Miss Potts said.

"This investigation is going to take a long time," Holt said.

"I know," Miss Potts said.

After lunch, they took a taxi to Lake Michigan. At the shoreline beach, people were sunbathing and swimming. Others were in rowboats and canoes.

"Miss Potts, can you swim?" Holt said.

"Yes, but I don't have a swimming suit," Miss Potts said.

"I wasn't thinking of swimming," Holt said. "More in the line of a rowboat or canoe."

"A canoe? This lake is larger than Rhode Island," Miss Potts said.

"Close to shore the water is very calm," Holt said.

Miss Potts looked at the canoes and rowboats puttering around close to the shoreline. "We can't go past those ropes," she said.

Holt nodded. "Let's go," he said.

After Cavill and Goodluck left to catch their train, Sato and Yuki sent the girls to the backyard so they could talk privately.

"You helped them, so why do you need to return to Chicago?" Yuki said.

"Springfield. And the job is far from finished," Sato said.

"But it is not your job," Yuki said. "You are an engineer, a builder of bridges and tunnels. You're not some policeman in a dime novel."

"Do you like living in San Francisco?" Sato said.

"It's a modern city with many advantages for the girls," Yuki said.

"You answered a question I did not ask," Sato said.

Yuki lowered her eyes for a moment and then looked at him. "No," she said.

"Neither do I," Sato said. "Springfield is a

small town with a lot of nice people, and the winter is not much different than back in Japan. At least give it a chance before you make judgment."

"When will you go?" Yuki said.

"When they send me a telegram," Sato said. "Within a week."

Yuki nodded. "You have become quite American since we left Japan," she said.

"How do you mean?"

"In Japan, a man would never ask what his wife thinks about anything," Yuki said. "He simply barks an order and it's followed."

"We are no longer in Japan, and I happen to value what my wife thinks," Sato said.

"We must start making arrangements if we are to move to Springfield," Yuki said.

Miss Potts felt a bit more secure in the rowboat over a canoe, so they rented one for an hour. Holt proved very capable with the oars. He rowed about fifty feet out to the ropes and several hundred feet away from the crowd.

In the distance they could see ships coming and going to the docks.

"Miss Potts, may I tell you what I plan?" Holt said.

"Certainly."

"I am going to leave my seat and sit next to you and kiss you," Holt said.

"You forget yourself, sir," Miss Potts said.

"I haven't forgotten that you're a woman," Holt said. "A very desirable woman who has stirred my blood since the day I came to work for the agency."

"Mr. Holt, watch your language," Miss Potts said. "You are not addressing a saloon girl."

"I am well aware of that," Holt said as he left his seat and sat next to Miss Potts.

"Charles never approved of . . ." Miss Potts said.

"Charles is gone, sad to say," Holt said. "And we are not."

"Oh, go on. Get it out of your system," Miss Potts said.

Holt leaned in close and kissed Miss Potts on the lips. To his delight and surprise, she returned the kiss with force and passion.

Then Miss Potts shoved Holt away, looked at him, and said, "Goodness."

"Should I apologize?" Holt said.

"Hell no," Miss Potts said. She grabbed Holt and kissed him.

"Why don't you quit early, go back to your hotel, and get some rest," Poule said. "The reports from your people won't be here for several days to a week, so there is no sense exhausting yourself."

"I think I will," Duffy said.

He took a cab from the Justice Department to his hotel and requested a shave and a bath before returning to his room.

After the barber shaved him, Duffy lit a cigar and soaked in a tub of hot water and oils.

At least a week before he returned to Springfield. There was no word from Kathy, but she didn't have ready access to a telegraph so he wasn't surprised.

Duffy closed his eyes and puffed on the cigar. Had he handled things the way Porter would have, had he lived?

He wanted to think so.

Weary, Duffy got out of the tub, toweled dry, dressed, and returned to his room to sleep.

"Did I please you?" Holt said.

"Very much so," Miss Potts said. "Twice, in fact. Blow out the lantern so we can get some sleep."

Holt reached for the lantern on the bedside table and blew it out. Instantly the room went completely dark.

Miss Potts put her head on Holt's chest.

"Lester?" she said.

"Yes?"

"This was the first time in a very long time for me," Miss Potts said. "I want you to know that."

Holt ran his fingers through her hair. "I'm glad it was with me," he said.

"As am I," Miss Potts said. "Get some sleep. You'll need your strength to please me again in the morning."

CHAPTER TWENTY-TWO

Sato was shocked when there was a knock on his door and Cavill and Goodluck were standing there.

"I thought you returned to Springfield," Sato said.

"A slight change of plans," Cavill said. "We thought we'd discuss it with you."

"Come in," Sato said. "Yuki will make some coffee."

Ten minutes later, Cavill, Goodluck, and Sato sat on the sofa in the living room with cups of coffee.

"We got to thinking yesterday when we were waiting for the train," Cavill said. "We could spend three days and nights traveling to the office only to sit around waiting for Jim, or we could head north to Portland and Seattle and check things out."

Sato nodded. "Very wise," he said.

"Are you coming with us?" Goodluck said.

"Excuse me for one moment," Sato said.

Sato went to the kitchen to speak with Yuki. He returned in ten minutes.

"Allow me some time to pack," he said.

Miss Potts unlocked the office door, entered, and lit several oil lanterns to brighten up the dark rooms.

Holt took a buggy to town for the mail. While he was gone, Miss Potts fired up the woodstove in the lunchroom and made a pot of coffee.

She took a cup to Duffy's desk, sat behind it, and waited for Holt. He finally arrived with an armload of mail, including telegrams from Duffy, Quill and Harvey, and Cavill.

Holt filled a cup with coffee and sat on the edge of the desk while Miss Potts read the telegrams.

Duffy would be in Washington for at least another week, awaiting all field reports.

Quill and Harvey would be in the office tomorrow morning.

Cavill, Goodluck, and Sato were going to Portland and Seattle to monitor the shipping ports. They would send word where to send a reply.

"Lester, do you want to go to California to help Cavill, Goodluck, and Sato with this investigation?" Miss Potts said.

"Who's Sato?" Holt said.

"He's the . . . never mind," Miss Potts said. "I think it's important that you go tomorrow, along with Quill and Harvey."

"That's three days on a train," Holt said.

"It is, yes."

"Let me cook dinner for you, and I'll go," Holt said.

"Dinner?"

"I'm handy in the kitchen," Holt said.

"I see," Miss Potts said. "Tell me, Lester, is the kitchen on your mind or the bedroom?"

Holt grinned. "Six o'clock. Don't be late."

In Poule's office, Duffy read the telegram from Cavill. "Who knew the big lug could actually think?" he said aloud.

At his desk, Poule looked up at Duffy. "Who?" he said.

"Jim Cavill," Duffy said. "Rather than return to the office and do nothing, he is going to Portland and Seattle to check their ports."

"He's the big one, right?"

"Yes. Do me a favor and send a telegram to the chief of police of Portland and the one in Seattle requesting their cooperation," Duffy said.

"I'll do that right now," Poule said.

■ ■ ■ ■

"Ever been to Portland before?" Cavill said.

"First time," Goodluck said.

"I designed a railroad bridge a couple of years ago in Portland," Sato said. "I spent about two months here."

Cavill and Goodluck left their horses at a livery near Sato's house in San Francisco and took a taxi to police headquarters.

Portland was a moderate-size town of about twenty thousand residents. Settlers in the 1830s first arrived using the Oregon Trail, and it grew at a slow but steady pace. Its access to the Pacific Ocean via the Willamette and Columbia Rivers helped advance growth quickly once ports were established.

The taxi took them to a large brick building on a street called Police Justice Center, adjacent to a courthouse.

Cavill, Goodluck, and Sato checked in with a desk sergeant in the lobby.

"The chief is expecting you," the desk sergeant said.

"He is?" Cavill said.

"A telegram from Washington arrived this morning," the desk sergeant said.

A uniformed officer walked them to the

second floor to the chief of police's office.

Chief Kinkade had spent his entire life in law enforcement. He started as a deputy sheriff in small western towns and migrated west, working as sheriffs and police officers up and down the West Coast.

"I received a telegram from Federal Prosecutor Poule in Washington about you men this morning," Kinkade said. "I have the general idea, but tell me everything you know."

"This could take a while," Cavill said.

"I'll have a man bring us some coffee," Kinkade said.

Duffy studied the map of the United States that hung on the wall in Poule's office. He had stuck pins in the locations where children had gone missing. East, west, north, and south, Valdez spared no part of the country.

Privateer ships for hire.

Men to transport the children.

How many hands to bribe.

"I was just thinking," Duffy said. "An operation like this requires money, and a great deal of it, to get started."

"I imagine so," Poule said from his desk.

"By all accounts, King Valdez is a small-time criminal," Duffy said. "Where did the money come from to start an operation like this? Someone way above Valdez is in charge."

"Yes, but who?" Poule said.

"Someone with a great deal of money and the knowledge to make an operation like this work," Duffy said.

"What are you leading up to, Jim?" Poule said.

"When we catch Valdez, if you want the man at the top, you're going to have to make a deal," Duffy said.

Chief Kinkade lit one of Cavill's Cuban cigars and said, "Tomorrow morning, I'll have two detectives take you to the waterfront with a warrant to search records."

"Not yet, Chief," Cavill said. "We'd like to do some surveillance work first. Can your people show us around for a location?"

Kinkade nodded. "I'd like to check that out myself. Can you be here at eight o'clock?"

"Eight o'clock," Cavill said. "By the way, can you recommend a hotel?"

Miss Potts went home, took a hot bath, and changed into fashionable evening clothes for her dinner appointment with Holt.

She took her personal buggy for the mile-

110

long drive to Holt's home. She parked in his yard, walked to the front door, and knocked.

Wearing a white apron, Holt answered the door.

"Why do I feel like a fly about to enter the spider's web?" Miss Potts said.

"Because you are," Holt said with a grin.

CHAPTER TWENTY-THREE

When Miss Potts opened her eyes, for a moment she forgot where she was. Then she remembered, rolled over, and shook Holt.

"Lester, wake up. We have to get to the office," she said.

Holt opened his eyes. "What time is it?" he said.

Miss Potts looked at the windup clock on the table beside the bed. "Not quite seven," she said.

"All right, stay in bed while I make some coffee," Holt said.

After Holt went to the kitchen, Miss Potts went to the washroom. She filled the basin with water from the pitcher and washed her hands and face and sponged off before dressing.

The coffee was ready when Miss Potts entered the kitchen.

"Want me to fix you some breakfast?" Holt said.

"Only when we're away from the office do I have breakfast, otherwise I take just coffee," Miss Potts said.

"I'd better shave and get dressed," Holt said. "I won't be long."

It was a bright, beautiful morning. Miss Potts took her coffee outside to the porch and sat in one of two chairs.

Something odd had happened to her, something she had given up on a long time ago. A man had entered her life. Not since her early twenties, when she fell in love with that good-for-nothing who left her at the altar, had she had feelings for a man.

Then along came Lester Holt.

Who came out to the porch at that moment with a cup of coffee and sat beside her.

"A fine morning," he said.

"Yes, it is," Miss Potts said. "Lester, are you using me?"

"What?" Holt said with shock in his voice.

"Are you using me?" Miss Potts said. "It's been done before, you know."

"Not by me it hasn't," Holt said. "Everything that's happened, everything I said, I meant every word."

Miss Potts looked at Holt. "Are you sure?" she said.

"I'm going to Seattle on your say-so and

for no other reason. Of course I'm sure," Holt said.

Miss Potts smiled. "We'd best get to the office," she said.

Quill and Harvey arrived at the office a few minutes before Miss Potts and Holt. They had their own key, entered, and made a pot of coffee. When the coffee was ready, Miss Potts and Holt walked in.

"You got our telegram?" Quill said.

"Yes," Miss Potts said. "Have you ever been to Seattle?"

"Seattle?" Harvey said.

"Pull up a chair, lads," Holt said. "This will take a while."

"I need to send a telegram to Mr. Duffy," Miss Potts said.

Duffy arrived at Poule's office to find a telegram waiting for him from Miss Potts.

Behind his desk, Poule said, "It just arrived not five minutes ago."

Duffy opened the envelope, sat in a chair, and read the telegram.

"Cavill, Goodluck, and Sato are in Portland. Quill, Harvey, and Holt are on the way to Seattle," Duffy said.

"I received replies from the chief of police in both cities," Poule said.

"I was up half the night thinking about the source of Valdez's front money," Duffy said.

"And?" Poule said.

"The entire operation is too organized, too complicated for a criminal like Valdez to have planned and executed," Duffy said. "Whoever is behind this is not only highly intelligent, but he's also skilled and wealthy."

"It takes money to make money," Poule said.

"Yes, but it's more than that," Duffy said. "Say you were wealthy, worth millions. Would you know how to organize an international smuggling operation that specializes in children?"

"No. I would not," Poule said.

"Neither would I," Duffy said. "It takes someone with experience."

"Everything we know about Valdez indicates he has none, or at least didn't in the past," Poule said.

"He has a mentor," Duffy said.

Miss Potts opened the safe, removed several thousand dollars in expense money, and handed it to Holt.

"I guess we better go home and pack clean clothes for the trip," Harvey said.

115

"I'll meet you boys at the depot at noon," Holt said.

"More trains," Quill said.

"It's the life, isn't it?" Holt said.

After Quill and Harvey left the office, Holt said, "I believe I'll steal me a kiss."

"Lester, we're in the office," Miss Potts said.

"I'll be gone a week or more," Holt said. "I'll need something to keep my spirits up on the long trip."

Miss Potts stood up from the desk. "Go lock the door," she said.

CHAPTER TWENTY-FOUR

From a rooftop a thousand yards away from the docks on the riverfront, Cavill, Goodluck, Sato, and Police Chief Kinkade kept an eye on the dock activity with binoculars.

"What happens at night?" Cavill said.

"I have no idea," Kinkade said. "It's locked down, I suppose."

"Security?"

"Most likely," Kinkade said.

"It's my guess that illegal activity happens at night," Cavill said. "We need to get closer so we can keep an eye on things after dark."

"Directly across from the docks is a building we can use," Goodluck said. "It says ironworks on the side, but it looks empty."

"Chief, can you get us on that roof without anyone knowing?" Cavill said.

After opening the mail, Miss Potts went to the bank and deposited checks totaling thirty-one-thousand dollars.

She grabbed a light lunch at the café near the office, then returned and sent a telegram to Duffy.

At her desk, she read the lists of requests from potential clients. There wasn't manpower available at the present time to handle any of them.

She sent another telegram to Duffy.

Duffy was looking at the map on Poule's office wall when Poule walked in with a large stack of mail.

"Packages from your men and three telegrams," Poule said.

Duffy went to the sofa to read the telegrams. Miss Potts had deposited thirty-one-thousand dollars in the bank. Her second telegram was about pending assignments there wasn't the manpower to accept.

The third telegram was from Cavill. They weren't going to check ships' manifests just yet. They were going to conduct night surveillance on the port before they checked manifests.

"Of course," Duffy said aloud. "Tom, I need to send a telegram."

"Something happen?" Poule said.

"I'll explain in a minute," Duffy said.

Duffy left the office to use the telegraph reserved for Poule in the next room. He sent the telegram to Miss Potts, telling her to wire Quill, Harris, and Holt and request they conduct the same nighttime dock surveillance in Seattle.

He returned to Poule's office and told him about the telegram.

"Good move on your people's part," Poule said.

"Let's open the reports," Duffy said.

Late in the afternoon, Duffy replied to Miss Potts's telegrams. He instructed her to have Quill, Harvey, and Holt do the same surveillance in Seattle as was being conducted in Portland.

Holt and the others wouldn't arrive in Seattle for at least another forty hours, so she would have to wait for them to contact her before sending them a telegram.

There was nothing left for Miss Potts to do except lock up the office and go home.

She took her buggy for the one-mile ride home. She put her horse in the small barn and saw to his needs before entering the house and lighting several lanterns.

The house was quiet. She'd never noticed just how quiet before.

She went to her bedroom to change, then the kitchen to see about something to eat for dinner.

119

She opened the four-drawer icebox to check around. She hadn't been shopping for a while and there was nothing much inside. Some eggs, bacon, peppers, milk, butter, cheese, and bread.

She emptied the drip pan and then loaded the stove with wood and made a fire. She put on hot water for a cup of tea and sat at the table to drink it.

So quiet, it was eerie.

"Oh, my God," she said aloud when she realized that she was missing Holt.

Pushing forty and you're missing a man. After all those empty years, she was missing a man.

And it felt good.

After dark, Cavill, Goodluck, Sato, and Kinkade came up from the rear of the two-story building and climbed the attached ladder to the roof.

They had a bird's-eye view of the ships docked at port.

A dozen lanterns on poles illuminated the walkway along the pier. Most of the ships were dark and quiet. The teamsters were long gone and most, if not all, crew from the ships were getting drunk in town.

"Who's watching this place?" Goodluck whispered.

"Apparently no one," Cavill whispered.

"Wait. Someone is coming," Goodluck whispered.

A man walked along the dark pier. He held a Winchester rifle loosely in his right hand. He wore a cap instead of a hat and was dressed like a dockworker. He patrolled more than walked. Each time he passed a ship, he gave it a quick glance.

"The night watchman," Kinkade whispered.

"Joseph, when he reaches the end, get out your watch and time how long it takes him to make a complete patrol of the pier," Cavill said.

They looked on as the night watchman walked to the end of the pier and turned around.

Goodluck looked at his watch. The night watchman walked slowly to the front of the pier and disappeared into the darkness.

"Three minutes," Goodluck whispered.

"How often does he patrol?" Sato said.

Fifteen minutes passed, and the night watchman didn't reappear.

"Joseph, can you sneak down there and see what that watchman is doing?" Cavill said.

"I'll do it," Sato said. "I trained for such things when I served in the Japanese Army."

Sato removed his shoes and jacket and then went to the ladder. "I won't be long," he whispered.

He silently descended the ladder to the grass behind the building.

After a minute, Kinkade whispered, "Do you see him?"

"No, but that's the point," Cavill said.

Ten minutes passed and then, silently, Sato climbed back over the ladder.

"There is a little shack at the front of the pier," he whispered. "He's sitting inside. I think he's reading a book."

"Give him some time, and we'll see when he makes another patrol," Cavill said.

The night watchman didn't appear again for two hours. Then made his rounds and returned to his shack.

"It's after midnight. Let's head out and meet for breakfast in the morning," Cavill said.

Sometime around one in the morning, Duffy sprawled out on the sofa in Poule's office and fell asleep.

Poule had left at midnight and urged Duffy to return to his hotel.

They had made a great deal of progress with mapping and documenting the field reports.

However, enough was enough and, exhausted, Duffy fell asleep.

CHAPTER TWENTY-FIVE

Duffy rolled off the sofa a bit after six a.m. He went to the washroom to shave and wash up, and then went downstairs to the cafeteria for a large mug of coffee.

He brought the mug back to the office, opened the drapes to let the sunlight in, lit a cigar, and returned to work.

Around eight-thirty, Poule walked into the office.

"My God man, have you been here all night?" Poule said.

"Yes. Look at this," Duffy said.

Poule went to the conference table where Duffy had been working.

"I've listed the ships in port at Chicago, Philadelphia, Saint Louis, Dallas, and San Francisco for the months the children went missing," Duffy said. "On the night the last child was reported missing in each city, a privateer ship was in port and sailed the next morning."

Poule looked at the documents and then at the map. Duffy had highlighted the ports in red.

"We have the names of these privateer ships," Duffy said. "Ask the president to have the Coast Guard be on the lookout for them."

Still bending over the map, Poule turned and looked at Duffy.

"Go back to your hotel, take a bath, put on clean clothes, and meet me here at noon," Poule said.

At breakfast Cavill, Goodluck, Sato, and Kinkade discussed strategy for the waterfront.

"We'd like to give it a week," Cavill said. "If nothing develops, we'll go in and take a look at the manifests."

"Boys, I'm a bit dog-eared to be sitting on rooftops all night, but I'll assign you two of my best detectives to work with you," Kinkade said.

"Fair enough," Cavill said. "Tell them to meet us at our hotel around six for dinner. Then we'll ride over to the pier."

After breakfast, Cavill and Goodluck decided to take a walk around Portland. Sato returned to the hotel to write a letter to his wife.

The main streets were crowded with shoppers, vendors, and carriages.

Although wearing firearms wasn't outlawed in Portland, Cavill and Goodluck seemed to be the only two wearing them.

"Look," Cavill said as they turned a corner.

Midway down the block was a boxing gym.

"Let's take a look," Cavill said.

The gym was called the Portland Boxing Club for Gentlemen. Cavill and Goodluck entered the gym and paused to look around.

Two rings were centered in the large room. Men were sparring in each ring. In one corner hung large sacks filled with sand that men were punching. Other men skipped rope, while others tossed medicine balls. On the opposite side of the gym, men lifted barbells.

"What are those?" Goodluck said.

"Bicycles," Cavill said.

"How come they're not moving?" Goodluck said.

"They're called exercise bicycles," Cavill said. "Come on, I need a little exercise."

"Jack, we . . ." Goodluck said, but Cavill was already walking away.

Cavill walked to the two rings where a group of men were seated in chairs. Several of the men smoked cigars.

"Is the owner of this gym present?" Cavill said.

A gruff-looking man in his sixties stood up. "That would be me. Who are you?" he said.

"My friend and I are passing through, and I wondered if I could use your gym for a bit of exercise," Cavill said.

"Fee is a dollar a day for guests," the manager said. "Twenty-five cents for a locker."

Cavill paid the manager two dollars.

"I don't make change," the manager said.

"Don't want any," Cavill said. "Joseph?"

Goodluck walked to Cavill. "Hold my things," Cavill said and removed his holster and gave it to Goodluck.

Cavill removed his jacket and shirt and tossed them to Goodluck. "Any chance I can spar a round?" Cavill said to the manager.

"You look like a big and powerful farm boy to me, son," the manager said. "Any experience in the ring?"

"Some," Cavill said.

"Hey, Clayton, get over here," the manager said.

A man almost as large as Cavill stopped punching a bag and walked to the manager.

"This man wants to spar a round," the manager said. "Don't pull your punches."

"Yes sir," Clayton said.

"Go on, farm boy," the manager said.

Cavill and Clayton stepped into the ring.

"Oh, farm boy, I don't know how they do it where you come from, but here a round ends when a man is knocked down," the manager said.

Cavill nodded.

"Time," the manager said.

Clayton rushed forward and attacked Cavill with several stiff jabs that Cavill blocked. Clayton tried a body shot to Cavill's stomach. Cavill sidestepped it and knocked Clayton unconscious with a powerful right hook to the jaw.

Cavill looked at the manager. "Is the round over?" he said.

"Who are you?" the manager said.

"Just a farm boy passing through," Cavill said.

Duffy and Poule spoke for about an hour. President Arthur listened and made notes with a pencil.

"It wouldn't be out of the ordinary for the Coast Guard to stop a ship leaving port for a surprise inspection, would it, sir?" Duffy said.

"It would not," Arthur said.

"Thank you," Duffy said.

"Mr. Duffy, has Tom offered you a position yet?" Arthur said.

"He has," Duffy said.

"And?"

"I told him I'll think about it after we catch Valdez," Duffy said.

Miss Potts sat at her desk and opened the mail. There was a check for twenty thousand dollars from the Montana Stock Growers Association from a previous case. There were also a half-dozen requests from other states and territories that needed help.

At the moment, there wasn't the manpower available to do the work.

She sent a telegram advising Duffy of the situation, and then she took a walk to the bank to deposit the check.

On the way back to the office, she stopped for lunch at the small café and read the newspaper as she ate.

When she returned to the office, she made a cup of tea. Duffy replied to her telegram as she returned to her desk.

Duffy said he would be returning to the office within a week and asked if Kathy had returned.

Miss Potts answered Duffy with: *No, she*

hasn't as yet.

"And I know just how you feel," she said aloud.

Cavill and Goodluck were having a small drink of whiskey on the sofa in the lobby of their hotel when Clayton and another man entered and walked to the desk.

Clayton and the other man spoke to the desk clerk, who pointed to Cavill and Goodluck.

"Hey, Jack, isn't that the man you knocked out this morning?" Goodluck said.

"It is," Cavill said.

"Maybe he wants a rematch?" Goodluck said.

Clayton and the other man approached Cavill and Goodluck.

"You got to be kidding me," Clayton said.

"If you want a rematch, I'll be happy to . . ." Cavill said.

Clayton took out his badge. "Chief Kinkade sent us," he said. "I'm Detective Clayton, and this is Detective Morris."

"Hungry?" Cavill said.

"Yeah, but I'll have to chew on the left side," Clayton said.

"One of the boys at the club said they saw you fight Sullivan one round in San Francisco a week ago," Clayton said. "He said you won the round."

Cavill sliced into his steak. "Someday soon we'll do it for real," he said.

"I believe you," Clayton said.

"About this assignment," Morris said. "What the chief said is frightening."

"And that's why we're going to spend the night on a rooftop," Cavill said.

CHAPTER TWENTY-SIX

After a long day of seeing patients, Kathy locked her door, made a cup of tea, and sat at the kitchen table to open her mail.

She wasn't expecting a letter from Jim. It would take a month or better if he did mail one, which he probably wouldn't because he was expecting her back in Springfield.

She didn't know which she wanted more, dinner or a hot bath.

She got neither.

There was a loud pounding on her front door. A boy's voice cried out, "Doc Bodine, it's my pa. He's terrible sick."

Kathy went to the door. The boy was about fourteen.

"It's my pa," he said. "He's sick something fierce."

"Calm down, son," Kathy said. "Who is your pa, where do you live, and what's wrong with him?"

"We live about five miles north and he cut

his leg about a month ago," the boy said. "It's swollen something awful."

"Who are you?" Kathy said.

"Josh Mason."

"All right, Josh, do you know how to hitch a buggy?"

"Yes, ma'am,"

"Go to my barn and hitch my buggy. I'll follow you to your house," Kathy said.

Kathy packed her bag with medicines and tools, tossed on a coat, and met Josh out front.

"I'll follow you," she said.

Forty minutes later, Kathy met Susan Mason in the living room of the farmhouse she shared with her husband and Josh.

"Tell me what happened," Kathy said.

"He cut his right leg on a rusty saw," Susan said.

"When?" Kathy said.

"About a month ago," Susan said.

"Boil water and a lot of it," Kathy said. "Where is your husband?"

Josh took Kathy into the bedroom. Mr. Mason was in bed, asleep and covered in sweat.

"Stand back, Josh," Kathy said as she removed the covers and examined the right leg.

Ten minutes later, she met with Susan and

133

Josh in the kitchen.

"I won't lie to you, Mrs. Mason. It's bad. Very bad," Kathy said.

"How bad?" Susan said.

"I have to remove the leg below the knee or he will die," Kathy said.

"When?"

"Right now, or he will be dead in two days," Kathy said.

Susan closed her eyes for a moment, then opened them and nodded.

"You and Josh will need to help me," Kathy said.

Shortly before dawn, Kathy and Susan sat in chairs on the porch with cups of coffee and watched the sun slowly rise.

"I don't know how we're going to run this farm without my husband being able to work," Susan said.

"In a month, I'll fit him for a prosthesis," Kathy said. "He'll learn to walk. In time be able to do anything he wants. In the meantime, you have a fine, strong son."

"I'm grateful to you, doctor," Susan said. "Very grateful."

"I'll be back tonight," Kathy said. "He'll sleep most of the day, but if he wakes up give him the medicine I left you, and he'll go right back to sleep."

134

Riding home, Kathy knew she wasn't going to return to Springfield.

CHAPTER TWENTY-SEVEN

After a night of watching the watchman make patrols every few hours, Cavill, Goodluck, Sato, Clayton, and Morris had drained the gallon pot of coffee they'd brought from the hotel.

"It will be light soon," Goodluck said. "We'd best be going before the dock workers arrive."

"Hold up," Cavill said. "Look."

The night watchman walked along the pier and stopped in front of a privateer ship. He took out a small notebook and pencil, jotted a few notes, then turned and walked back to his shack.

"Write down the name of that ship," Cavill said.

Clayton took out his notebook and made a notation.

"Let's get out of here," Cavill said.

Over breakfast at the hotel, Cavill said,

"That privateer ship was marked for a reason."

"In two nights, that watchman never even looked at another ship," Goodluck said.

"We should see Chief Kinkade and let him know," Clayton said. "We might need more men."

"We have enough," Cavill said. "Tonight bring your rifles and extra ammunition."

Clayton and Morris exchanged quick glances.

"What?" Cavill said.

"We . . . we've never had to actually fire our weapons in the line of duty before," Clayton said.

"The line of duty?" Cavill said.

"What he means is . . ." Morris said.

"I know what he means," Cavill said. "Well, don't worry about it. Chances are there will be no shooting."

Clayton nodded. "We better tell the chief anyway," he said.

"You do that, but remember, we don't need any more men," Cavill said.

Seattle was a major port city in the territory of Washington. Talk was that Washington would soon be admitted to the Union as a state.

The city itself was fairly small, with just

137

six thousand residents. Almost every able-bodied male worked at the docks in one form or another.

Shipbuilding was a major factor, as was acting as the gateway north to Alaska.

Although Seattle was the northernmost city on the West Coast, the climate was mild even in winter and never really got hot in summer.

Quill, Harvey, and Holt walked through muddy, wagon-clogged streets to the Central Hotel to book rooms.

"This place ain't much," Holt said as they entered the lobby of the hotel.

"We need three rooms," Quill told the desk clerk. "And a bath. You have a barber?"

An hour later, after being shaved by the hotel barber, Quill, Harvey, and Holt soaked in tubs of hot, soapy water.

"Kind of late to see the police chief tonight," Holt said. "We'll get a fresh start in the morning."

"We should wire the office and let Miss Potts know we arrived," Quill said.

"Right before we get something to eat," Harvey said.

Miss Potts was about to leave the office when the telegraph clicked with an incoming message. She rushed to the key, tapped she was ready, and then copied the message from Seattle.

Quill, Harvey, and Holt had arrived in Seattle.

Miss Potts carefully replied with Duffy's instructions.

The reply came within a few minutes. *Message received.*

After that, she sent a telegram to Duffy in Washington.

After Duffy replied to Miss Potts, he sat on the sofa in Poule's office.

"I need to get back," Duffy said.

"When?" Poule said.

"Tomorrow."

"If I can swing it with the boss, I'd like to go with you," Poule said. "I need to get out of the office more."

Duffy grinned. "Pack heavy," he said.

CHAPTER TWENTY-EIGHT

Joey Jordan sat at her desk in the den of her ranch house and read the adoption papers given to her by the lawyer in Helena.

Although the lawyer explained in detail the process and read every word to her, the procedure was complicated and difficult to understand.

Nearly a year ago Cavill had ridden up to her ranch house with two orphans: Adam, who was twelve; and his sister, Sarah, who was just ten. Their parents were murdered, and in the course of whatever investigation Cavill was mixed up in at the time, he rescued Adam and Sarah and brought them to her for safekeeping. She couldn't imagine not having them at this point in her life.

Cavill had stayed with her for several weeks until he left to help find the man who had murdered his partner's future wife.

It had been months, and he hadn't returned.

She gave up hope he ever would.

Jack Cavill was not a man to be tied down to a ranch. He was a man of action who loved pursuing criminals. Hauling fence and driving cattle would break his spirit. She saw that now.

She hoped he had received her last letter by this time, but he probably hadn't.

"Adam, Sarah, could you please come to the den," Joey called out.

They had become so much a part of her life now that it felt as if they had always been part of it.

They appeared in the den.

"Yes, Joey?" Adam said.

He was a shy boy, but was slowly gaining confidence.

"Have a seat on the sofa," Joey said.

"Did we do something wrong?" Sarah said.

"No, sweetheart," Joey said. "I just want to explain a few things to you, okay?"

Adam and Sarah sat on the sofa. Joey stood with the adoption papers in her hand.

"Do you remember when we went to town a few days ago, and I went to see the lawyer?" Joey said.

"We remember," Adam said.

"I went to see him about legally adopting the both of you," Joey said. "Do you know

141

what that means?"

"No," Adam said.

"No, ma'am," Sarah said.

"It means that I can legally adopt you as my children, and I will legally be your mother," Joey said. "My question to you is, do you want that?"

The question was answered with hugs, kisses, and crying.

"Okay then," Joey said. "We'll go to town tomorrow and file the papers."

CHAPTER TWENTY-NINE

"Is that a bow and arrow?" Clayton said as he ascended the ladder behind Goodluck.

Once they were all on the roof, Cavill said, "Joseph can take out your eye at fifty yards in the dark with that thing."

The sky was darkening quickly. Cavill leaned over the roof and pulled the rope tied to the gallon caldron of hot coffee below and brought it to the roof.

Each man dunked his cup into the caldron and Goodluck replaced the lid.

Besides the bow and arrow, Goodluck had a sack on his back that he set aside.

"What's in the bag?" Cavill said.

"A dozen biscuits from the hotel, a pound of jerky, and chocolate bars," Goodluck said.

"Chocolate bars?" Clayton said.

"I got a sweet tooth," Goodluck said.

"Here comes the watchman," Sato said.

Holding a torch and a step stool, the watchman stopped at every lantern and lit it for the evening. When he reached the end of the pier, he turned around and walked back to his hut.

"Best get settled in," Cavill said.

"Footsteps," Goodluck whispered.

They leaned over the edge just enough to see. The watchman and two men dressed as longshoremen walked along the pier.

They stopped in front of the privateer ship and chatted softly for a few moments.

Then the watchman turned and walked back to his shack. The two longshoremen went aboard the ship and were gone for about ten minutes. Lights came on below deck, then they reappeared on deck with cups of coffee.

Each of the longshoremen lit cigarettes.

"Joseph, can you take them out from here?" Cavill whispered.

"No problem," Goodluck whispered.

"Clayton, Morris, after Joseph takes them out, board the ship, put on their jackets, and stay in the shadows," Cavill whispered. "And for God's sake, be quiet about it."

Goodluck removed two arrows from his pouch, loaded the first one, and took aim. The arrow struck one man in the neck and he fell to the deck. The second man turned to look at the first man and Goodluck's second arrow tore his throat away.

Cavill turned to Clayton and Morris. "Go," he whispered.

Clayton and Morris silently descended the ladder, crossed the pier, and went aboard the privateer ship.

"And now we wait," Cavill whispered.

An hour passed. The watchman made his rounds. He waved to Clayton and Morris on the dark deck of the privateer ship. They waved in return. Then the watchman went back to his patrol.

Another hour passed, and voices sounded from the end of the pier near the watchman's shack.

"I'm going down," Cavill said. "Joseph, Sato, get ready."

Cavill went over the edge and descended the ladder. He stayed behind the building with his Winchester at the ready.

Voices grew louder.

Footsteps sounded.

Two men plus the watchman led six young girls along the pier. The girls were crying.

"Shut up, or you'll get what for," one of the men said.

The two men and watchman stopped the girls in front of the privateer ship.

"Get them on board and be quick about it," the watchman said.

An arrow struck him in the back, and he went down.

Cavill rushed out and cocked the lever of his Winchester. "Five rifles aimed at your heads," he shouted. "You girls, come over here."

The six girls ran to Cavill's side.

Clayton and Morris walked the gangplank to the pier and stopped at the two men. "You men are under arrest," Clayton said.

The two men had sidearms.

"Go ahead, reach for them," Cavill said. "I haven't killed anybody in a while, and I'm sort of anxious."

The rescued girls sat in a coach at the end of the pier. Cavill, Goodluck, and Sato watched as Clayton, Morris, and a dozen uniformed officers searched the privateer ship.

Police Chief Kinkade stood beside Cavill.

"Who put the arrow in the watchman's back?" Kinkade said. "And the two on the ship?"

"Goodluck," Cavill said. "Three hundred feet in the dark."

Kinkade looked at Goodluck. "How did we ever defeat you?" he said.

"We defeated ourselves," Goodluck said.

"Clayton, Morris, let's get these kids

home and the two suspects in custody to the station for questioning," Kinkade said.

"Wait," Cavill said. He grabbed one of the suspects. "What time is the ship supposed to set sail?"

"Why should I tell you anything?" the suspect said.

"Because if you don't, I'm going to beat you to death and toss your body in the ocean," Cavill said. "I promise you that."

"Six o'clock," the suspect said. "But we weren't sailing with them. Our end was just to deliver these kids."

"How and why?" Cavill said.

"We're pickup crew," the suspect said. "We sign on for a month's work to those that need extra hands. We were having a beer in the sailor's pub, and this man asked us to deliver those young girls to the pier."

"And just like that, you did?" Cavill said.

"He paid us two hundred dollars," the suspect said. "That's more than a month's wages at sea."

"There better be a captain and crew here in two hours, or I keep my promise," Cavill said. "Chief Kinkade, I suggest everybody get out of sight."

A dozen uniformed police officers hid on board the privateer ship. Kinkade, Clayton,

Morris, Goodluck, Sato, and the remaining police officers took up positions behind the building across from the privateer ship.

Cavill wore the watchman's jacket, although it was too small to button. He waited in the shack at the end of the pier.

At the first hint of sunlight in the sky, a dozen men came from the street and walked past Cavill onto the pier.

Cavill let them get a good head start, and then he followed them from a distance. As they approached the privateer ship, Cavill sped up and closed the distance to about twenty feet.

Cavill waited for them to step onto the gangplank. Before they could board the ship, a dozen of Kinkade's men appeared.

The dozen men backed up.

Cavill drew and cocked his Colt. "The back door is closed," he said. "I suggest you surrender peacefully or be prepared to take a swim in Davy Jones's locker."

CHAPTER THIRTY

The captain of the privateer ship insisted on making a deal for himself before he would give up any information.

Portland had only a small courthouse, one judge, two prosecutors, and two defenders.

A prosecutor named Kelly arrived at the police station at eight-thirty in the morning and met Kinkade in his office.

"I think you should get the full story from the men who planned this operation from the beginning," Kinkade said.

"Where are they?" Kelly said.

"They went to send a telegram," Kinkade said. "They should be here momentarily."

Before leaving their hotel, Quill, Harvey, and Holt stopped by the desk where a fresh telegram waited for them from Miss Potts.

Holt read the telegram. "Change of plans," he said and showed Quill and Harvey the telegram.

"What time is it back in Springfield?" Holt said.

"Eight-thirty," Quill said.

"Let's get some coffee, wait until nine, and respond to Miss Potts," Holt said.

Miss Potts sat at her desk with a fresh mug of coffee. She was about to send a telegram to Duffy when the key clicked to life.

She grabbed a pencil and copied the message from Cavill. Once she finished writing she had to read the message twice. Then she sent a telegram to Duffy, replied to Cavill, and then sent a fresh telegram to Holt.

Duffy entered Poule's office a bit after ten in the morning.

"I checked out, Tom," Duffy said. "Are you ready to go?"

"Just packing up my briefcase," Poule said.

"Train leaves at noon. We can have lunch in the dining car," Duffy said.

An aide rushed into the office with a telegram. "I thought you'd want to see this right away," he said.

Poule took the telegram, read it, and passed it to Duffy.

"Well, Tom, it looks like we're catching the train to Portland," Duffy said.

"I'll send a telegram to the police chief

150

before we go," Poule said,

At the conference table in Kinkade's office, Cavill, Goodluck, Sato, Clayton, and Morris spoke to Kelly for more than two hours.

"We want Valdez," Cavill said. "I'm sure the chief agrees with us on that point."

"We all agree on that, but I can't give away the store on a possibility," Kelly said.

"These men are responsible for saving a half-dozen young girls from a life of slavery," Kinkade said. "I'd say it's worth giving up a little something to save a lot more, wouldn't you?"

"There are hundreds of missing kids out there," Cavill said. "Sold into slavery. They deserve to be rescued, don't you think?"

"Where is the captain?" Kelly said.

Quill, Harvey, and Holt checked the hotel desk, and the clerk handed Holt a new telegram from Miss Potts.

"All right, let's go see the police chief," Holt said.

They took a taxi to police headquarters about one mile away.

The police chief, Paul Coffey, met them in his office. He was close to sixty, a career law-enforcement man who had worked a dozen cities and towns along the western seaboard.

"Our people arrested a privateer captain about to smuggle six young girls out of the country," Quill said. "And it's probably happened here in Seattle right under your noses."

"I received a telegram from Chief Kelly in Portland," Coffey said.

"Let's take a ride to your docks," Holt said. "Bring men. Lots of men."

Kinkade and Kelly sat across a table from the privateer captain in the interrogation room.

"Have you come to deal or to waste my time?" the captain said.

"You're facing life in federal prison, Captain," Kelly said. "You're forty-two years old. That's a long time behind bars."

"I walk, or you can kiss my Irish ass," the captain said.

"We both know you're not going to walk, Captain," Kelly said. "Ten years is my offer in exchange for what you know."

"Like I said, kiss my Irish ass," the captain said.

"Do you think I'm bluffing here?" Kelly said.

"Do you?" the captain said. "Imagine all those parents out there grieving over their missing children, you had the opportunity get them back, and you didn't because you didn't want to make a deal. Can you see the headlines in the newspapers? I can. Some terrible things they'll say about you and your court system."

"You can rot in jail for the rest of your miserable life," Kelly said.

There was a knock on the door and Kinkade went to answer it. Cavill held a telegram. "I think you both better see this," Cavill said.

Kinkade and Kelly stepped out of the room, read the telegram, and then returned to the captain.

"In three days a federal prosecutor from Washington will be here," Kelly said. "You can make your deal with him."

Cavill, Goodluck, Sato, Clayton, and Morris had a late lunch at the hotel dining room.

"It looks like we've got nothing to do the next three days until Jim and the federal prosecutor get here," Cavill said.

"Speaking for myself, I'm going to sleep for the next twelve hours," Sato said.

"Clayton, how often do you visit that boxing gym?" Cavill said.

"Several times a week," Clayton said.

"How about tomorrow?" Cavill said.

153

"As long as I don't have to spar with you," Clayton said.

"Sato, why don't we rent some horses and take a ride in the country?" Goodluck said.

"I'd like that," Sato said.

"Let's get some dessert," Cavill said.

CHAPTER THIRTY-ONE

"See here, Captain, you can't do this," the harbormaster said.

"Can't I?" Coffey said. "I have twenty armed police officers and a warrant signed by a judge that says I can. Order every man to stop working and get off the pier, or you and they go to jail."

Quill, Harvey, and Holt stepped forward. "His logbook," Quill said.

"And your logbook," Coffey said to the harbormaster.

Cavill and Clayton warmed up by working the heavy bag at the Portland Boxing Club for Gentlemen.

"Anybody worth a spit fighting in this place?" Cavill said.

"Not in your class," Clayton said.

"Let's find out," Cavill said.

Cavill and Clayton walked across the gym to where the manager was seated in a chair outside the ring. Two fighters were sparring in both rings.

"You again," the manager said. "What do you want?"

"I want to fight, what else?" Cavill said. "I'm not here for cooking lessons."

"I know who you are," the manager said. "After the other day, I did some checking. You fought a round with Sullivan in San Francisco. Some people say you won that round pretty handily."

"I like to keep in shape," Cavill said. "You got any fighters willing to go one round?"

"How many do you want?" the manager said.

"Say five," Cavill said. "Any man on his feet after one round gets ten dollars."

"Make it twenty, and we'll take side bets," the manager said. "You lose if any man makes the round on his feet."

"Get the five men," Cavill said.

"This is some beautiful country, this Oregon," Goodluck said.

After breakfast, Goodluck and Sato rented horses from a livery stable near the hotel and rode east out of Portland. The countryside was lush and green, with massive Douglas fir trees and Ponderosa pines just about everywhere.

156

They paused beside a stream that ran off the Columbia River.

Goodluck smoked his pipe as they sat against a tree.

"Tell me about Japan," Goodluck said.

"It's the size of California," Sato said. "Mostly warm, but the northwest gets snow in winter. It's entered the modern era the past twenty years. The samurai are gone, and modern armies protect the emperor. Although traditions and culture are strictly adhered to."

"Will you go back?" Goodluck said.

"No," Sato said. "For all of its faults, in America I have to bow to no one."

Goodluck nodded. "Things have changed a great deal in America the last fifty years," he said. "When I was a boy, I rarely saw a white man. As a young man, I fought many wars against them. Now I live and work with them. The slaves are free, and I read that some of them are now serving in Congress."

"This country will be great one day," Sato said. "One day it will lead the world."

The first three fighters lasted less than thirty seconds against Cavill. The fourth made it to sixty seconds, mostly by backpedaling and running until Cavill caught up to him with a powerful right hook.

Before he entered the ring, the manager called the fifth fighter aside and rubbed pepper juice on the cloth wraps around his fists.

"Get a jab anywhere near his face and blind the son of a bitch," the manager said.

The fifth fighter nodded and climbed into the ring.

"Time," the manager said.

The fifth fighter charged Cavill and jabbed several times. Cavill blocked the jabs but the fumes from the pepper juice immediately caused his eyes to water.

Cavill recognized the fumes. "Bastard," he said.

The fifth fighter tried to land a few jabs to Cavill's eyes. Cavill grabbed the fifth fighter by the waist, lifted him in the air, and tossed him out of the ring.

"You son of a bitch," Cavill yelled. He jumped out of the ring and grabbed the manager.

"Pepper juice," Cavill said. "I ought to —"

Clayton grabbed Cavill. "Take it easy, Jack," he said. "You made your point."

"I can't abide cheating," Cavill said.

"Neither can I," Clayton said. He looked at the manager. "Pay all bets, or spend the night in jail."

■ ■ ■ ■

Quill, Harvey, and Holt checked the log-book for every ship into and out of the port for the previous thirty days.

More than a dozen privateer ships had come and gone in that span.

"What privateer ships are in port right now, Chief?" Quill said to Coffey.

"Four," Coffey said. "The *Grace,* the *Jewel,* the *Elizabeth,* and the *Sea Master.*"

Holt looked at the list. "All four have been here before in the past thirty days."

"Let's check them," Quill said.

Coffey, Quill, Harvey, and Holt returned to the docks, where Coffey ordered his men to search the four privateer ships.

"Chief, the dock workers are getting impatient," a uniformed officer said.

"Have the men keep them at bay," Coffey said.

Three of the four privateer ships were loaded with cargo bound for Alaska, Southern California, and Mexico.

The fourth ship, *Elizabeth,* had little to no cargo, but had a dozen cots set up below deck.

"What do you suppose these tiny cots are intended for?" Coffey said. "Smuggling children, do you think?"

"It appears so," Quill said.

"Find the captain of this ship," Coffey said.

The captain of the *Elizabeth* was nowhere to be found.

"I want six officers on board this ship until the Coast Guard arrives and hauls it away," Coffey said. "And you, Mr. Harbormaster, are under arrest."

"For what?" the harbormaster said.

"Bribery, for a starter," Coffey said.

"Chief Coffey, might I suggest we check the missing persons' reports for children from the Washington area," Quill said.

Coffey nodded. "Yeah," he said. "That's exactly what we will do."

CHAPTER THIRTY-TWO

"Nine reports on missing children in the territory of Washington," Coffey said. "Several right here in Seattle."

"Any word of the captain and the crew of *Elizabeth*?" Holt said.

"No, but I have all available manpower on the street," Coffey said.

"Chief, have the bars searched, especially those near the waterfront," Holt said. "Somebody knows something."

Cavill received the telegram from Seattle when he returned from the boxing gym. Goodluck and Sato were still out riding around the countryside, so he would break the news to them over dinner.

He took a shave before a hot bath, then returned to his room for a nap. He slept for about an hour, dressed, and went down to the desk and sent a telegram to Joey.

Goodluck and Sato had returned by then.

Cavill showed them the telegram from Seattle when they grabbed a table in the hotel restaurant.

"Good work," Goodluck said. "I hope they find the ship's captain and crew."

"May I suggest something?" Sato said. "Why don't we go to Seattle and assist them? It's only a few hours on the train."

"That's not a bad idea," Cavill said. "You and Joseph go. I'll stick around and wait for Jim."

"We can check the train schedule at the front desk," Sato said.

Teams of detectives covered the bars and saloons in the downtown and waterfront districts of Seattle.

Harvey, Quill, and Holt went with a team of four detectives and covered bars and saloons near the waterfront.

There were dozens of them. Every one was filled with thirsty crew members from ships at port.

Ale, beer, and whiskey flowed like water. Every bar had prostitutes and hustlers and recruiters for new crew members.

Most of the clientele were drunk or on their way to it.

"We've been at this for hours," Quill said. "If that captain and his crew were at the docks this morning, they are long gone."

"I agree," one of the detectives said.

"Let's have us a drink and get the hell out of here," another detective said.

Harvey, Quill, Holt, and the four detectives found a table and ordered beer.

"Let's face it, lads," a detective said. "We might never find that captain."

"We have to," Holt said. "Missing children are at stake."

A dark-haired prostitute approached the table and took a vacant chair next to Quill. "How are you lads tonight?" she said.

"Lady, we're the police," a detective said.

"I know that," the prostitute said. "I'm not here to wiggle your beans."

"Then what do you want?" Harvey said.

"You want information on a certain ship's captain," the prostitute said. "I have information on a certain ship's captain. But, like my button hole, it ain't free."

"What ship?" Quill said.

"*Elizabeth,*" the prostitute said. "That you get for free."

"Look, lady, missing kids are at stake here," Holt said.

"I know that," the prostitute said. "I saw them."

"You saw them?" a detective said.

"That's all you're going to get for free,"

the prostitute said.

"How much?" Quill said.

"Five hundred, and I'll take you to them," the prostitute said.

"Let's go," a detective said.

"Where?" the prostitute said.

"To get your money," a detective said.

Chief Coffey, woken from a sound sleep, dressed and reported to his office shortly after one in the morning.

"Is this the lass?" Coffey said when he entered the interrogation room.

"I'm your lass," the prostitute said. "For five hundred dollars."

"Take me to him," Coffey said. "And you'll get your money."

The flophouse was located about a quarter of a mile from the waterfront. It was a two-story, wood-frame building with a balcony on the second floor.

Lanterns glowed from several windows on both floors.

Coffey had the police paddy wagons park a block from the house. Then he and twenty officers, plus Quill, Harvey, and Holt, walked to the house.

"Are you sure this is the house?" Coffey said.

"I serviced them for two days. I'm sure," the prostitute said. "The kids were on the second floor in bedrooms."

"All right men, we go in loaded for bear," Coffey said. "Shoot if you have to, but I want the captain alive. Half take the front door. The rest take the rear. Let's go."

Coffey led his men to the front door where two men swung a battering ram made from a log and smashed in the door.

At the same time, the officers at the back door smashed it in and rushed into the house through the kitchen.

A dozen men inside the house were caught off guard, and the officers had little trouble subduing them.

"I want the captain of the *Elizabeth*," Coffey said.

The dozen apprehended sailors kept quiet.

"I'll say it another way," Coffey said. "Eleven men have to do minimal time of three months if you give up the captain. Otherwise, you all do life."

"Him," a sailor said and pointed to a gruff-looking man of about forty. "That's him."

"Excellent," Coffey said. "Now where are the kidnapped children?"

"Basement," a sailor said.

■ ■ ■ ■

"Doctor, how are the girls?" Coffey said.

"They'll sleep until morning," the doctor said. "More scared than hurt."

"My detectives will come by in the morning and take their information. We'll see they get home safely," Coffey said.

"Chief, let's get some breakfast," Quill said. "We have something to discuss with you."

"I guess it is breakfast time. Why not?" Coffey said.

Quill, Harvey, and Holt rode in Coffey's personal coach to the hotel, where they had breakfast in the restaurant.

They ordered ham, eggs, potatoes, toast, and coffee.

"Tomorrow sometime a federal prosecutor will be arriving in Portland to prosecute the case against the ship's captain apprehended with kidnapped children on board," Quill said. "Why not let him prosecute the captain of *Elizabeth* as well. It would carry far more weight on the federal level."

"I agree," Coffey said. "It would."

"We'll send word to our people in Portland right after breakfast," Harvey said.

"No need," Holt said.

Goodluck and Sato approached the table, "The desk clerk said you were in here," Goodluck said.

"Chief Coffey, two of our people from Portland," Quill said.

"Sit down. Order some breakfast," Holt said. "We have some good news to share."

An hour later, over coffee in the hotel lobby, Coffey said, "I'll hold the captain of the *Elizabeth* and allow you men to take him to Portland for the federal prosecutor to deal with."

"He arrives tomorrow," Goodluck said. "He'll telegraph you to release the prisoner to our custody."

"I'll be waiting," Coffey said. "Right now I'm going to the office, and then home for some sleep."

"Sounds like a good idea," Quill said.

"You men do excellent work," Coffey said before parting.

After Coffey left, Goodluck said, "We'd better wire Jack and Miss Potts."

CHAPTER THIRTY-THREE

After breakfast in the hotel dining room, Cavill stopped by the desk to find a telegram from Goodluck waiting for him.

He read the telegram, then went outside and hailed a passing taxi to take him to police headquarters.

Chief Kinkade had just arrived and was having coffee in his office when Cavill knocked on his door.

"Enter," Kinkade said.

Cavill opened the door, walked in, and set the telegram on the desk.

Kinkade read it quickly and looked up at Cavill. "Two of them in the fry pan now. One of them must know where Valdez is hiding."

"Chief, I'd like for you and me to meet the train tomorrow morning at ten," Cavill said.

"A little pomp and circumstance might be in order," Kinkade said. "Meet me here at nine-thirty tomorrow morning, and we'll pick them up in my coach."

"The captain, has he said anything yet?" Cavill said.

"Just that he won't talk without a deal that lets him walk," Kinkade said.

Cavill nodded. "See you at nine-thirty tomorrow," he said.

Miss Potts read the telegram from Goodluck. The news about the rescued children was grand. Duffy and the prosecutor would have their hands full when they arrived in Portland tomorrow.

She was tempted to take the train and join them, but somebody had to man the office.

Besides, she wasn't sure if she wanted to go to help with the case or to see Holt.

She decided to wait for instructions from Duffy.

Goodluck, Sato, and Holt rented horses and took a ride in the countryside. Washington, like Oregon, was lush green forests with tall pine trees and Douglas firs.

After several hours, they stopped to rest the horses in the shade of some tall pines.

Goodluck lit his pipe, Holt smoked a cigar.

"There's something on my mind, boys," Holt said. "And hear me out before you pass

169

judgment."

"Go on," Goodluck said.

"I like this country," Holt said. "Maybe not Seattle or Portland, but it's still growing and has lots of potential. I was thinking we should approach Jim and suggest we open a branch office out here. Maybe San Francisco or Sacramento. It's time for the agency to grow and expand with the times. Well, what do you boys think?"

"It's true that a business needs to grow to stay competitive," Sato said. "I am in favor of it."

"Joseph?" Holt said.

"I go along with that," Goodluck said. "It would be easier to travel to the western states from here rather than Springfield."

"We'll run it by Quill and Harvey over dinner," Holt said.

Quill and Harvey spent the afternoon in the hotel billiards room. There were two standard billiards tables and two pool tables.

They played several games at both tables.

"You know, I wouldn't mind settling out here," Quill said.

"It would be a change," Harvey said.

"Of course, we'd have to resign our positions and start over," Quill said.

"I like what we do," Harvey said. "I really

don't want to do anything else right now."

"Well, let's get cleaned up for dinner," Quill said. "The others should be back from their ride by now."

"A branch office. That's a fine idea," Quill said. "We should have thought of it a long time ago."

"It's up to Jim now," Goodluck said. "But I think he'll see the merit in the idea."

"We'll find out soon enough," Holt said. "As soon as we take the prisoners to Portland tomorrow morning."

CHAPTER THIRTY-FOUR

Duffy and Poule stepped off the train in Portland to find Cavill and Chief Kinkade waiting for them beside Kinkade's coach.

"Jack, good to see you," Duffy said as he shook Cavill's hand.

"Jim, this is Chief Kinkade," Cavill said.

"Nice to know you, Chief," Duffy said. "This is Tom Poule from the Justice Department."

"Let's get going," Kinkade said. "We have much to talk about."

"Everybody concerned has done an outstanding job," Poule said. "They should have my telegram by now in Seattle to release the other ship's captain. In the meantime, I'd like to talk to this one."

"He's waiting in our interrogation room," Kinkade said.

"Chief, I'd like you and Jim in the room with me," Poule said.

A few minutes later, Poule, Duffy, and Kinkade sat across a table from the captain of the privateer ship. He looked at them as he smoked a rolled cigarette.

"I'm Tom Poule of the Justice Department," Poule said.

"I don't care if you're Lillie Langtry, the Jersey Lily, so long as you get me out of here," the captain said.

"You don't really think you're getting off without doing some time?" Poule said.

"You want Valdez, you give me what I want," the captain said. "And what I want is to walk away a free man."

"You don't seem to understand, Captain," Poule said. "You were caught red-handed trafficking in children for sale outside the United States. That's life at hard labor if you don't get hung. You're in no position to bargain."

"You got that backwards, friend," the captain said. "I'm holding the winning hand. I have what you want, and the price ain't cheap."

"We shall see," Poule said. "Another privateer captain was arrested in Seattle. Caught red-handed like you. He's being transported to Portland. I'm going to offer him the same deal. Whoever takes it gets one year. Whoever doesn't gets a rope."

"You're bluffing," the captain said.

"It's your neck that's going to get stretched," Poule said and stood up. "We're done here."

Poule, Duffy, and Kinkade walked to the door.

"Hey, wait," the captain said just as they walked out.

Poule, Duffy, Cavill, and Kinkade went to lunch at a restaurant near the railroad station so they could pick up Quill, Harvey, Goodluck, Sato, and the prisoner.

"Between one of them, we'll get Valdez," Poule said.

"What if they both give him up?" Cavill said.

"First come, first saved," Poule said.

"What's the news on the children?" Duffy said.

"Hear they were treated at the hospital and are being returned to their homes," Kinkade said.

"The same in Seattle," Quill said.

"You men have saved more than twenty children and potentially many more," Poule said. "You're to be commended."

"What we want is Valdez," Cavill said. "He killed Mr. Porter in cold blood, and he should swing for that."

174

"Mr. Cavill, we want justice, not revenge," Poule said.

"Sometimes they're the same thing," Cavill said.

"Jack, now is not the time," Duffy said. "We can discuss that after we find out where Valdez is holed up."

Cavill nodded. "The train should be here by now," he said.

"Tom, this is Mr. Quill, Mr. Harvey, Joseph Goodluck, and Mr. Sato," Duffy said. "Boys, this is Tom Poule of the Justice Department."

Poule looked at the man in irons. "And you must be the captain of the *Elizabeth*," he said.

"I'll make the same offer I made to the other captain we have in custody," Poule said to the captain of *Elizabeth*. "Give me King Valdez in exchange for one year in a federal prison. If you don't, you'll most likely be hung."

The other captain must have turned it down if you're talking to me," the captain of *Elizabeth* said.

"Get it through your head, you're not going to walk," Poule said. "One year is very generous. Otherwise, you swing."

The captain of *Elizabeth* nodded. "What do you want to know?" he said.

"Everything," Poule said.

CHAPTER THIRTY-FIVE

The meeting was moved to Kinkade's office where Poule, Duffy, Kinkade, and the captain of *Elizabeth* sat at the conference table.

"What are we waiting for?" the captain of *Elizabeth* said. "I'm ready to talk if you're ready to put your deal in writing."

"My secretary," Kinkade said. "She should be here momentarily."

A few moments later there was a knock on the door and she entered. She held a notepad and pencils in her hand and took a seat.

"Note the date and the time," Kinkade said.

The secretary scribbled in shorthand.

"All right, Captain, from the beginning," Poule said. "How you met Valdez, what he paid you, and what you did for him."

"Maybe three months ago in spring, I met Valdez in a bar on the waterfront."

"The name of the bar?" Poule said.

"The Gypsy Rose," the captain said.

"I know the place," Kinkade said. "It's a hangout for crew in port. I spent several years as a captain in Portland."

"Go on," Poule said.

"Me and my crew had just returned from running a shipment of rum from Barbados to Portland and were waiting on another job. There is always somebody wants something shipped from here to there. There's a man there almost every night. He acts as a go-between, so to speak. He arranges jobs for private ships like mine. He said he had a new client with big money he wanted me to meet."

The captain of *Elizabeth* paused to light a rolled cigarette.

"And?" Poule said.

"And we went to the back room, and I met King Valdez," the captain of *Elizabeth* said. "He said he was interested in hiring a ship to take a shipment of guns to a political group that wanted to overthrow the United States of Colombia."

"I've heard of that," Poule said. "Go on."

"I took the job for fifteen thousand dollars," the captain of *Elizabeth* said. "Thirty crates of rifles and whatnot to Colombia. A month at sea and when I returned, I met

178

with Valdez and he paid me and offered me another job. Thirty thousand to take eight kids to Tortuga."

"Tortuga?" Poule said. "There's nothing there. Are you sure it wasn't Haiti?"

"My instructions were to meet another ship and transfer the kids at Tortuga."

"Bound for where?" Poule said.

"I was never told."

"And?"

"And I returned to Portland, got my money, and Valdez told me to stick around, he'd have another shipment for me," the captain of the Elizabeth said.

"That's when you were intercepted?" Poule said.

"Yes."

"You were bound for where?" Poule said.

"I don't know. Valdez never got the chance to tell me because you people arrested me," the captain said.

"All right, where can we find Valdez?" Poule said.

The captain of the privateer ship laughed as he rolled another cigarette. "I'm not stupid, Mr. Justice Department man," he said. "You get Valdez when I get my deal in writing."

"Agreed," Poule said. "But the deal begins when Valdez is captured. Give me ten minutes to draw up the papers."

Duffy stopped by the lunchroom where Cavill and the others were having coffee.

"What the hell is going on, Jim?" Cavill said.

"Tom is preparing the agreement," Duffy said.

"It better be a good one," Cavill said.

"I need to get back," Duffy said. "I'll fill you in later."

"Here is your agreement," Poule said. "Read it carefully."

The captain of *Elizabeth* took the document from Poule, read it, and then said, "Got pen and ink?"

Poule produced a pen and a bottle of ink and set them on the table.

After the captain of *Elizabeth* signed the agreement, Poule said, "Now for your end of the bargain."

"We have to go back to Seattle," the captain of *Elizabeth* said.

"Don't fool with me, Captain," Poule said. "I'll tear up that agreement and you'll swing."

"I'm not fooling," the captain of *Elizabeth* said. "By Valdez's orders, one of my crew was one of his men. It was his insurance we wouldn't cheat him. The man couldn't sail worth a damn. Point is, the man knows exactly where Valdez hides out when he isn't working. You want him, we go to Seattle, I give him to you, and you get Valdez."

Poule nodded. "We go to Seattle," he said.

CHAPTER THIRTY-SIX

"We just came from Seattle," Quill said.

"We don't all need to go," Duffy said. "Jack and I can go with Tom. The rest can wait for us to return with the prisoners."

"From what I hear, Miss Potts could use some help at the office," Holt said. "Maybe I should go back and give her a hand?"

"Good idea," Quill said. "Harvey and I should go too."

"Yes, she must have other assignments waiting," Duffy said.

"We'll take the train in the morning, but first there is something else we wish to discuss with you, Jim," Quill said.

"It's about the office," Harvey said.

"What about the office?" Duffy said.

"Well, we think it's time we expanded," Holt said. "Opened a branch out here on the West Coast. Maybe in Sacramento."

Duffy looked around the dinner table. "I take it you all feel that way," he said.

"It's time, Jim," Cavill said.

"I guess it is at that," Duffy said. "As soon as this Valdez business is concluded, we'll make plans for expansion."

"We'll wire Miss Potts in the morning and let her know we'll be returning to the office," Holt said.

"Here comes Mr. Poule," Sato said.

Poule took a vacant seat at the table. "I wired Washington and gave them an update," he said. "So, what's good for dinner?"

After dinner, Duffy, Cavill, Poule, and Goodluck played pool in the hotel billiards room. Besides the pool and billiards tables, there were several card tables, and Sato, Quill, Harvey, and Holt played poker.

"The eight o'clock train gets us into Seattle at noon," Poule said as he banked a shot. "There is a four o'clock train returning. I'd like to be returning with a bird in hand. Once the US Marshals take over and . . ."

"What?" Cavill said. "Who said anything about US Marshals?"

"I assumed you knew the marshals would take over and apprehend Valdez," Poule said.

"You assumed wrong," Cavill said. "Valdez murdered Porter in cold blood. We're not going to bow out of this and let some

183

Washington bureaucrat tell us what to do."

"Jack, that's enough," Duffy said.

"I agree with Jack," Goodluck said.

"As do I," Sato said.

"We all do, Jim," Quill said. "It's only right."

"How about it, Tom?" Duffy said. "Joseph is the best tracker in the country, and Jack is worth ten marshals."

Poule sighed. "It will have to be a shared venture between your people and mine," he said.

"I can live with that," Duffy said. "Jack, Joseph, can you?"

Cavill looked at Poule. "Just don't send some Washington bureaucrat who thinks it's a field trip away from the office," he said.

"Two top men," Poule said. "The best in the department."

Cavill lined up a shot and banked it into a corner pocket. "They better be," he said. "Valdez will shoot first and talk later."

"Just remember one thing," Poule said. "We want Valdez alive."

Cavill lined up another shot and banked it. "Tell that to Valdez, because he's not going to want to talk first," he said.

After dinner, Duffy, Cavill, and Goodluck brought small glasses of whiskey onto the porch of the hotel. Cavill and Duffy lit cigars, Goodluck smoked his pipe.

"Jack is right about one thing, Jim," Goodluck said. "When we get out there, it is no place for a derby-wearing dandy, badge or no badge."

"Tom is a good man, and he knows what he's doing," Duffy said. "More important, we know what we're doing. We've carried dead weight before and managed."

"I hope you're right," Cavill said. "Children's lives might depend upon some of that dead weight."

"So who got the idea of expanding the office west?" Duffy said.

"I think we all did sort of at the same time," Cavill said.

"Well, we'll have to take a trip to Sacramento when this is over and see if it's suitable," Duffy said.

"Mr. Porter would approve," Cavill said.

Goodluck raised his glass. "To Mr. Porter," he said and tossed back his drink.

CHAPTER THIRTY-SEVEN

After introducing Poule and Duffy to Police Chief Coffey, Poule explained the situation to him.

"Well, which of the crew is the man we want?" Coffey said.

"That's for the captain to decide," Duffy said. "Jack and Joseph are holding him in the interrogation room."

"Let's ask the man," Poule said.

"You want me to betray Valdez? Are you insane? He will have me killed for a betrayal like that."

His name was Miguel Lopez and, like Valdez, he was Mexican.

"Mr. Lopez, you don't seem to understand the situation you are in," Poule said. "For your part in this child-trafficking scheme, you will get twenty years in a federal prison. If you cooperate, you will do one year in a minimum facility. Otherwise you will be a very old man before you see the light of day again."

"Your captain understands," Duffy said. "That's why he brought us to you. Now you have a choice to make. Twenty years or one."

Lopez took a deep breath and then sighed. "Do you know the Sonoran Desert?" he said.

"A bit," Duffy said. "We have a man who knows it well."

"Valdez has a camp in the Sonoran," Lopez said. "Well protected by the mountains. There is even a freshwater spring. You'll never find it alone."

"We realize that," Duffy said. "Why do you think we are talking to you?"

"I take you to Valdez and I get one year instead of twenty?" Lopez said.

"Yes," Poule said. "And I'll sweeten the pot. I will consider the time spent traveling to Valdez as part of the year."

Lopez nodded. "I will take you to Valdez," he said.

"I will draw up the agreement for you to sign," Poule said. "Can you write your name?"

"I read and write very well," Lopez said. "In English and Spanish. And French. My mother was a schoolteacher in Texas after it became a state."

"I'll draw up the paper for you to sign within the hour," Poule said.

"Phoenix is the closest we can get to the Sonoran by train," Goodluck said. "After that we ride."

"I can't say as I've been there," Duffy said.

"It's ninety square miles, but only a third is actually in the US," Goodluck said.

"So Valdez could have his camp in Mexico?" Cavill said.

"It's possible," Goodluck said. "If he's willing to risk the *federales.*"

"We'll need authorization papers from Poule to cross over into Mexico," Duffy said.

"Wherever Valdez is holed up, it's not likely we'll run into any *federales,*" Goodluck said.

"But it's good to have it just in case," Duffy said. "So, who's been to Sacramento?"

"I know Sato has," Cavill said. "He designed a bridge for the Western Pacific."

"He didn't return to Springfield," Goodluck said. "He went to San Francisco to see his family and get our horses. He'll meet us here in Seattle."

"He's a good man, but a bit green for the desert," Duffy said.

"Remember how we met him?" Cavill said.

"He's as tough as nails, Jim," Goodluck said.

"All right, he comes with us," Duffy said. "Right now I have to get back to Tom."

Lopez read the agreement carefully and signed his name in ink.

"The time it takes to find Valdez comes off my year?" Lopez said.

"That's what you just agreed to by signing that agreement," Poule said.

"That's good," Lopez said. "Can I have some dinner now?"

"What would you like?" Poule said.

"Steak with potatoes and a vegetable and a glass of milk," Lopez said.

"Milk?" Duffy said.

"My mother taught me the importance of a healthy diet," Lopez said. "She said milk is good for your bones."

"Jim, get out the map while I go see the cook," Poule said.

Poule left the interrogation room while Duffy opened his briefcase and took out a folded map of Arizona.

"Show me on this map where Valdez hides out," Duffy said.

Lopez studied the map for several minutes. "Here," he said and pointed with his finger.

"The Arizona Mountains Forest?" Duffy said.

"Yes."

"Why on earth would Valdez pick that place for a hideout?" Duffy said.

"Who would be *loco* enough to cross the desert to get there if you didn't have to?" Lopez said.

"And you know the way?"

"Yes, I do," Lopez said.

Duffy packed up the map and stood. "Enjoy your steak, Mr. Lopez," he said. "And milk."

Chapter Thirty-Eight

Duffy, Cavill, Goodluck, Poule, and Chief Coffey went to dinner at the hotel restaurant.

"Joseph, do you know the Arizona Mountains Forest?" Duffy said.

"I do," Goodluck said. "Southeast of the Sonoran Desert."

"We'll leave when Sato arrives tomorrow with your horses," Duffy said. "I'll need horses for me and Lopez. Chief, where can we get fitted?"

"Abe's Livery usually has some good horses for the army," Coffey said.

"We'll check it out in the morning," Duffy said.

Cavill and Goodluck grinned at Duffy.

"What?" Duffy said.

"You're going to cross the desert and ride into the mountains dressed like an eastern banker?" Cavill said.

"I brought a set of trail clothes and my

sidearm," Duffy said. "I'll pick up a Winchester when we get supplies in Phoenix."

"We'll need a mule," Goodluck said.

"We'll get that in Phoenix," Duffy said.

"I hope you men know what you're doing," Coffey said.

"So do we," Duffy said.

"I know this may sound ridiculous, but I almost wish I was going with you," Poule said.

Everybody looked at Poule.

"Councilor, when was the last time you rode a horse?" Cavill said.

"I . . . took lessons," Poule said. "As a child. Back in Boston."

Cavill, Duffy, and Coffey grinned.

"Don't you worry about it, Mr. Poule," Goodluck said. "When the missionaries taught me to read and write many years ago, they said the pen was mightier than the sword. We carry a sword, but you carry the pen."

"Why, Joseph, I do believe you are a poet at heart," Duffy said.

Duffy, Cavill, and Goodluck sat in chairs on the porch at the hotel. They had small glasses of whiskey. Duffy and Cavill smoked cigars, Goodluck his pipe.

"Quill and the others should be back in

the office tomorrow morning," Duffy said. "I'll wire Miss Porter with our plans."

"Sato should be here in the morning with our horses," Cavill said.

"Joseph, tell us what you know about the Sonoran Desert," Duffy said.

"It's the hottest desert in the country, but different than the others," Goodluck said.

"Different how?" Cavill said.

"Most deserts get one season of rainfall but the Sonoran gets two," Goodluck said. "It's hell during the day and cold at night. Phoenix and Tucson are actually smack in the middle of it and exist only because of the two wet seasons. When we reach Phoenix, we got a long, hot ride to the Arizona Mountains Forest. It's no place for a dandy, that's for sure."

Poule stepped out from the hotel to the porch, holding a telegram. He took a chair beside Duffy.

"I just received this telegram from my office," Poule said. "It will be a week before two US Marshals can report to me in Seattle."

"Buy them lunch and wish them luck," Cavill said. "Because we'll be gone six days before they get here."

"I understand how you feel but a week isn't going to . . ." Poule said.

"Yes, it is," Duffy said. "You can't expect us to sit on our hands when we have the opportunity to hunt Valdez down and bring him in. The longer we wait, our odds of finding him grow smaller."

"The Justice Department . . ." Poule said.

"Hired us," Duffy said. "So let us do our job. Write out the authorization papers in case we need to enter Mexico, and we'll be off in the morning."

Poule sighed.

"We'll go anyway," Cavill said. "Papers or no papers."

"All right, I'll fill out the authorization papers," Poule said.

"Want to go with us?" Duffy said.

"No thanks," Poule said. "Those riding lessons I took didn't include deserts."

"Let's go to the bar and have a nightcap," Duffy said.

CHAPTER THIRTY-NINE

After Sato arrived with the horses, they walked them to Abe's Livery. There, Duffy picked out a horse for himself and one for Lopez.

Goodluck, the most qualified tracker, made the selections. Duffy paid three hundred dollars for two horses and saddles.

"We'll be back at three to catch our train," Duffy told Abe. "Feed and water them, but not too much."

Over lunch at the hotel, they told Sato the plan.

"I walked for many days through the prairie without food or water; I can just as easily ride a horse through the desert," Sato said.

"Let's go then," Cavill said. "We don't want to miss our train."

After boarding the horses in the boxcar, Duffy, Cavill, Goodluck, Sato, and Lopez dropped their gear off in their sleeping cars and then met in the gentlemen's car.

Some men were playing cards, and the pool table was occupied. They took a vacant table and ordered five drinks.

"What time do we arrive in Phoenix?" Cavill said.

"If we're on time, around eight p.m. tomorrow," Duffy said. "We'll stay over, get what we need for the trip, and head out in the morning."

Lopez took a sip of his drink. "How come I am not handcuffed?" he said.

"Because if you tried anything stupid, my partner Jack here would snap you like a dry twig," Duffy said.

Lopez looked at Cavill. "I believe you," he said.

"Let's talk about Valdez," Duffy said. "First thing is, can you find his hideout?"

"I know the way," Lopez said.

"And what will we find there?" Duffy said.

"A cabin, a corral, and an outhouse," Lopez said. "It's for emergency use."

"How many men?" Duffy said.

"Eight. Sometimes more. He knows things went bad. He'll hide out for a while," Lopez said. "He would have brought many supplies, and water is not far away."

"Who gives him his orders?" Duffy said.

"That I don't know," Lopez said. "Nobody does but him. What I can tell you is he leaves for a month at a time and takes two men with him. He rides south into Mexico, and when he returns there is a job to do."

"Who makes the arrangements for the privateer ships?" Duffy said.

"Not him," Lopez said. "Valdez is what you call a . . . how do you say man in the middle?"

"A middleman," Duffy said.

"Yes, a middleman," Lopez said. "When Valdez returns from Mexico, he gives the orders to his men and they go do the job. Sometimes he goes with them, sometimes not."

"How much do you get paid?" Duffy said.

"One thousand American dollars for each child," Lopez said. "Except for me. I never took a child. My job is to sail with the ship to make sure there is no cheating or harming of the children."

"And why is that?" Duffy said.

"I was in the Mexican Navy. I know ships," Lopez said.

"If you had to guess, what is Valdez doing right now?" Duffy said.

"Waiting for new orders," Lopez said. "He will ride south and return with them soon, if he hasn't done it already."

"How many such raids on children are you aware of?" Duffy said.

"In total, close to three hundred children," Lopez said. "But that's just a guess."

"What kind of a man are you?" Cavill said. "Steal kids from their families. I ought to throw you off this train headfirst through the window."

"Jack, cool off," Duffy said. "Valdez is the goal, remember?"

Cavill stood up and looked down at Lopez. "I hope you get out of line," he said and left the gentlemen's car.

Lopez looked at Duffy. "If he kills me, you will never find Valdez," he said.

"He won't kill you," Duffy said. "Despite his size and temper, Jack is a very smart man and knows the law."

"Joseph, how about a game of chess?" Sato said.

"Why not?" Goodluck said.

Goodluck and Sato moved to the chess table.

Duffy took a sip of his drink. "Mr. Lopez, if you do what we ask, give us no problems, and take us to Valdez, you will be a free man within one year. Young enough to start a new life and die of old age." Duffy paused to puff on his cigar. "But if you do decide to cross us up in any way, well, then I'm going to let Jack have his way with you. That is something you don't want to experience. That said, do we have an accord?"

"Dying of old age is better than being thrown off a speeding train," Lopez said.

"It certainly is," Duffy said. "Let's have another drink to whet our appetite for dinner."

CHAPTER FORTY

In the dining car, steaks were ordered all the way around.

"This business of expanding the office, it has potential," Duffy said. "And I think Sacramento is a good choice. But who goes to Sacramento to find and open the new office?"

"Quill and Harvey seem very keen on the idea," Goodluck said.

"I as well," Sato said. "We dislike San Francisco and Sacramento is more suited to my wife and children."

"Well, Mr. Sato, when we're done with this assignment, you go to Sacramento and find us a suitable office," Duffy said. "Quill and Harvey will be assigned to the new office, but we'll need at least six more agents and an office manager."

"And a tracker," Goodluck said.

"You know all the scouts in the army, Joseph. Find us one," Duffy said.

Goodluck nodded.

"You know, finding top men isn't going to be easy," Cavill said. "They need to know forensics, ballistics, be handy with weapons, and single men, to boot."

"Let's talk about that rule," Duffy said. "Mr. Porter made that rule because he didn't want to create widows and orphans, but I think it's outdated. Mr. Sato is married and I'm thinking about it myself, so let's vote on it. Yes or no. Yes, it stays. No, we get rid of it."

All agreed the rule would go.

"About recruiting good men," Duffy said. "There are ex-army officers and US Marshals tired of working for fifty dollars a month. When we started, what did we know about this kind of work? Nothing until Mr. Porter taught us, so that's what we'll do: teach them."

"We don't have to get fat and go grey in the hair, do we?" Cavill said.

"I'm already grey," Goodluck said.

"As am I," Sato said.

"That's what shoe polish is for," Cavill said.

Duffy picked up his wine glass. "Gentlemen, to new ventures," he said.

Cavill, Goodluck, and Sato held up the new glasses.

"To new ventures," Cavill said.

Lopez lifted his glass. "I have no idea what you are talking about but *salud*!" he said.

In the gentlemen's car after dinner, Duffy opened the map at a table after buying a round of drinks.

"On the map, it appears we have to cross about sixty miles of desert southeast to reach the Arizona Mountains Forest," Duffy said to Lopez.

"That is so," Lopez said.

"Then how long to Valdez's camp?" Duffy said.

"Two days to the east," Lopez said.

"I can't believe Valdez would go through this every time he needs to hide out for a while," Duffy said.

"He doesn't," Lopez said. "He will come north through the back door pass."

"Mexico?" Duffy said.

"It doesn't matter how he gets there so long as he's there," Cavill said.

"Two assignments went bad," Lopez said. "Much money was lost along with ships and men. He knows the law is after him now. He will be there."

"You said something about a back door," Cavill said. "Does he post lookouts?"

"Usually no," Lopez said. "There is no

202

need. He might now, but only during day-light. Nobody could track through those mountains at night."

Duffy and Cavill looked at Goodluck.

"Nobody?" Cavill said.

Lopez tossed back his drink. "I should warn you men," he said. "Valdez will hang in Mexico and he will hang in America. He won't go without shooting."

"That's our problem," Cavill said. "Your problem is getting us to him."

"At the moment my problem is I wish to get some sleep," Lopez said.

Duffy looked at Cavill. "He's in your car, Jack," he said.

"Let's go, Lopez," Cavill said.

"I think we all could use some sleep," Duffy said.

Cavill's car had two beds, two chairs, a table and a wash-up station, and a place to hang clothing.

After Lopez removed his boots, shirt, and pants, Cavill cuffed his right arm to the bed frame.

Then Cavill removed his boots, pants, and shirt, got on the floor, and did push-ups.

"What are you doing?" Lopez said.

"This is how I get ready to go to sleep," Cavill said. "Now shut up."

Lopez sighed and rolled over as best he could. "You people are very strange men," he said.

Chapter Forty-One

When they stepped off the train in Phoenix just after seven in the evening, the temperature was ninety degrees.

"You've got to be kidding me," Cavill said.

"Wait until noon, when it's a hundred and ten in the shade," Lopez said.

"Why would anybody build a town in this hellhole?" Cavill said.

"Let's find a hotel," Duffy said.

"Follow me," Lopez said. "I have been here many times."

They followed Lopez through the dusty streets. Mexican music played in several saloons. They drew stares from men in front of shops and saloons as they passed by.

"Hold up," Duffy said. "That general store is still open. Might as well place our order tonight so it's ready come morning."

"Stay with the horses," Cavill said as he and Duffy entered the store.

"Getting ready to close, gents," the man

behind the counter said.

"We won't be long," Duffy said. "We need supplies for five men for ten days. Beans, bacon, flour, sugar, coffee, baking powder, fresh meat, canned fruit, one bottle of whiskey, and plates, cutlery, and cookware. Cornbread if you have any fresh. And enough firewood to last."

"Crossing the desert, huh?" the man said.

"I need a Winchester and several boxes of ammunition," Duffy said. "And do you have gallon canteens?"

"I do," the man said. "A dollar a canteen to fill them up."

"We'll need eight," Duffy said. "Jack, you need anything?"

"A box of cigars and a pouch of pipe tobacco," Cavill said.

"I can't have all this until morning," the man said.

"We'll pay for it now and pick it up after breakfast," Duffy said.

"It comes to one hundred and eleven dollars," the man said.

Duffy paid the man and said, "We need a mule."

"Livery's at the end of Main Street," the man said.

"See you in the morning," Duffy said.

Duffy and Cavill returned to the street.

"All right, Mr. Lopez, we need a hotel," Duffy said.

Lopez led them to the Old House Hotel a few streets away from the saloons.

After checking in, they boarded the horses at the hotel livery next door. The restaurant in the hotel was still open and they grabbed a table.

The special was steak with potatoes, carrots, and beans, with apple pie for dessert.

"We'll get a mule and head out after breakfast," Duffy said. "Mr. Lopez, how are the nights in the Sonoran?"

"As hot as the days are, the nights are just as cold," Lopez said. "The desert doesn't hold the heat like it does here in town."

"Glad we brought our bedrolls," Duffy said.

"What do we do with the others?" Cavill said. "They're likely to fight before they surrender."

"Let them go," Duffy said. "We want Valdez, not them."

"We might have to kill some of them to make our point," Cavill said.

"Then we kill them, but if we kill Valdez, we would have taken a long trip through a hot box for nothing," Duffy said.

"Lopez, you know these men," Cavill said. "Are they fighters or cowards?"

"They would kill their mothers for a dollar," Lopez said. "But they are not stupid men. They won't die for no good reason."

"So we reason first," Duffy said. "But without Valdez, it's a wasted trip. So let's be careful who we shoot."

After dinner, they took glasses of bourbon onto the porch. Duffy and Cavill lit cigars, Goodluck smoked his pipe.

The temperature had cooled off about ten degrees to around eighty.

Sheriff Matt McCoy and two of his deputies approached the hotel and climbed up to the porch. The deputies carried shotguns.

"Evening, gents. I'm Sheriff Matt McCoy, and these are two of my deputies," McCoy said.

"How do you do, Sheriff," Duffy said.

"I don't believe in wasting time, so I'll get right to it," McCoy said. "Some folks in town are concerned you fellows might be bounty hunters. Bounty hunters means shooting and killing, and I don't want either in my town."

"We're not bounty hunters, Sheriff," Duffy said. "I'm reaching into my pocket for some papers. Have a seat and give them a read."

McCoy took the papers and sat in the vacant chair beside Duffy. He read quickly, flipping pages.

"I've read the bulletins put out by the Justice Department on the Valdez, but I never thought he was this close," McCoy said.

"We'll be leaving in the morning," Duffy said.

"I wish you luck," McCoy said. "Crossing the Sonoran is no easy task."

"We'll make it," Duffy said. "And we'll be back this way to take the train."

McCoy stood up. "I have a feeling you will," he said. "Good night, gents."

After McCoy and his deputies left, Duffy looked at Lopez. "Valdez has never been to Phoenix?" he said.

"Valdez is a very smart man when it comes to being seen," Lopez said. "It is easy to hide in a big city and not so easy in a small town."

"We got a long ride in the morning, I suggest we get some sleep," Duffy said.

"I have a request," Lopez said. "The big man kept me awake half the night doing his push-ups. Can I share someone else's room?"

"I should have warned you about that," Duffy said.

"He can bunk with me," Goodluck said.

"If my reading a book won't keep him awake."

CHAPTER FORTY-TWO

After purchasing a mule, as well as grain for it and the horses, Duffy walked the mule to the general store where the others waited with the horses.

Supplies and water were loaded onto the mule evenly. The supplies weighed less than the average rider on a horse.

"Lead the way," Duffy told Lopez.

Lopez led the group east and slightly south out of town. At ten in the morning the temperature was ninety degrees.

At two in the afternoon, with the temperature exceeding one hundred degrees, they rested for an hour.

"Wet the horses down a bit, but don't let them drink," Goodluck said. "Give them a carrot stick. That will keep them going until dark. If you must drink, no more than half a cup per man."

"You know the desert, huh?" Lopez said to Goodluck.

"At one time or another I have been in every desert in the country, including this one," Goodluck said. "Jim, you and Jack keep that white Irish skin of yours covered up real good."

After the hour passed, Lopez again led the group southeast until one hour before dark.

"Don't let the horse drink until after dark, but give them a good brushing," Goodluck said. "The mule, too."

Cavill built a fire with the wood they'd purchased, and he and Duffy got dinner started. Fresh beef with beans and potatoes and slices of cornbread. Cavill carefully measured out the water so that each man got one full cup.

After dark, before eating, they tended to the horses and mule.

The temperature dropped thirty degrees from the high at two o'clock, but it was still too warm to keep the fire going.

"We need to make twenty miles tomorrow," Duffy said. "Best get some sleep."

Sato went to remove his boots.

"Best keep them on," Goodluck said. "Scorpions like to sleep in your boots at night."

"They pack a punch," Duffy said. "Keep your boots on."

"Right," Sato said.

As they settled in to sleep, the stars came out, and the nearly full moon rose in the night sky.

In two nights the moon would be full.

Stopping for a one-hour rest, Duffy checked the maps. Lunch was cans of fruit with slices of cornbread and one cup of water per man.

"This desert is most unusual," Sato said. "I expected nothing but sand, like the Mojave, but there are many types of plants and vegetation here. And that cactus is most unusual."

"Those are part of the agave family," Goodluck said. "Over there, those are related to the palm, and those cactus are called saguaro cactus. This desert is the only desert in the world where it grows."

"How long were you in this desert?" Cavill said.

"Long enough to learn one cactus from another," Goodluck said.

"Well, let's get moving," Duffy said.

"Hold up," Goodluck said. "I see something from the northeast."

"I don't see anything," Cavill said.

Goodluck pointed. "Dust," he said.

Duffy got his binoculars from a saddlebag.

213

"It's dust all right, and moving toward us," he said.

"Who would be crazy enough to be out in this hellhole?" Cavill said.

"Besides us?" Duffy said.

"Best get ready for them," Cavill said and grabbed his Winchester from the saddle of his horse.

Duffy, Goodluck, and Sato took their Winchesters from their saddles.

"What about me?" Lopez said.

"You stand behind your horse and shut up," Cavill said.

Duffy kept watch with the binoculars. "I don't believe it," he said and handed the binoculars to Cavill.

"Soldiers," Cavill said. "Buffalo Soldiers."

"What are Buffalo Soldiers?" Sato said.

"All black soldiers," Duffy said. "It started during the war when freed or escaped slaves joined the army. They are some of the best soldiers in the country."

"But what are they doing here?" Cavill said.

"I guess we'll find out in a few minutes," Duffy said.

Slowly, six Buffalo Soldiers rode into view, riding in no particular hurry until they reached the camp.

One soldier, the one leading the other five,

wore the rank of sergeant major. He looked at Goodluck. "Chief Scout Joseph Goodluck, I haven't seen you in five years," he said.

Everybody lowered their Winchesters.

"Sergeant Major Titus Welding," Goodluck said. "What in blazes are you doing out here?"

Welding dismounted. "Looking for you," he said. "Dismount," he said, and the five soldiers dismounted.

"Looking for us?" Duffy said.

"Colonel Stafford at the fort north of Tucson received a telegram from a Tom Poule of the Justice Department requesting we accompany you across the desert," Welding said.

"That sneaky son of a . . ." Cavill said.

"Jack," Duffy said.

"Let's see now," Welding said. "You must be James Duffy," he said and nodded to Duffy. "The big fellow has to be Jack Cavill. No mistaking Mr. Sato. Where is your prisoner?"

"Come on out, Lopez," Cavill said.

Lopez stepped out from behind his horse.

"I don't suppose it would do any good to tell you we don't need an escort," Duffy said.

"I have my orders," Welding said.

215

"Escort us across the desert," Duffy said. "And after that?"

"My orders state to escort you across the desert," Welding said.

"Well, let's get going," Duffy said.

Welding turned to his five soldiers. "Mount," he said.

After dark, once the horses and mule were taken care of, they sat down to eat a supper of beef, beans, cornbread, and coffee. The Buffalo Soldiers had their own supplies and added some flavor to the beans with bits of bacon.

"I'm surprised to see you still in uniform," Goodluck said to Welding.

"Not for much longer," Welding said. "Twenty-two years in this man's army is enough."

"You joined during the war?" Duffy said.

"In sixty-three I ran away from the Welding Plantation and joined the Union Army," Welding said. "I was with the 54th out of Massachusetts, and later joined the Buffalo regiment in sixty-six with the 9th Cavalry. Been in ever since."

"May I ask you a question?" Sato said.

"Sure," Welding said.

"Your name is the same as the plantation," Sato said.

"I was born a slave on the plantation forty-three years ago," Welding said. "It's the only name I've ever known. Welding had a cousin named Titus. I was named after him, I suppose."

"Not exactly America's finest hour, Mr. Sato," Duffy said.

"The army has been real good to me," Welding said. "I retire with a pension, and I'm still young enough to do something with my life besides wear this uniform."

"You've given it some thought," Goodluck said.

"I thought I might try Boston," Welding said.

Two pots of coffee rested in the fire. "Let's sweeten the coffee a bit," Duffy said and removed the bottle of bourbon from his saddlebags.

"Those mountains you see in the distance, that's the forest," Lopez said. "When we reach them, we leave the desert behind and have another day's ride to the pass."

"I hope it's cooler in those hills than this frying pan," Cavill said.

Lunch was beans with bacon and corn-bread, with a touch of bourbon in the beans for flavor.

Duffy looked at his watch. "Lopez, we

have five hours to dark. Can we make those hills by then?" he said.

"Just about," Lopez said.

"Let's finish lunch and push on," Duffy said.

After everybody was mounted up, Lopez led the way.

"Buffalo Soldiers, how about a song to pass the time?" Welding said.

The five soldiers broke out in song:

We're fighting bulls of the Buffaloes. Git a going, git a going. From Kansas plains we'll hunt our foes a trotting down the line. Our range spreads west to Santa Fe, git a going, git a going, from Dakota down the Mexican way a trottin' down the line. Going to drill all day, going to drill all night. We got our money on the Buffaloes, somebody bet on the fight.

"Right pretty singing, Sergeant Major," Cavill said.

"We'll sing you right to those mountains," Welding said.

CHAPTER FORTY-THREE

They made camp in the early foothills of the Arizona Mountains Forest.

"My God, shade," Cavill said.

"It's that white Irish skin of yours," Welding said, "sucks up heat like a woodstove."

"Lopez, how far to the pass from here?" Duffy said.

"Tomorrow night early, we be there," Lopez said.

"Any water on the way?" Duffy said.

"We'll reach a spring by noon," Lopez said. "Fresh."

After tending to the horses and mule, they fixed a supper of beef, beans, cornbread, and coffee. Dessert was a treat of canned fruit.

"Titus, what's in Boston?" Goodluck said.

"I don't rightly know," Welding said. "But when I was there in sixty-three there were many Negros living there as free men and women. It seems like a place I might just fit into."

"And do what?" Goodluck said. "All you know is soldiering."

"I got a decent enough education in the army," Welding said. "And I'm a capable person. I can learn something new. You did. So can I."

Around the campfire, Duffy studied the map. "Lopez, this is the pass here to the east, is that correct?" he said.

Lopez looked at the map. "Yes. Tomorrow night we reach here," he said.

"And from the pass to Valdez is how long?" Duffy said.

"Half-day's ride," Lopez said.

Duffy looked at Goodluck, and Goodluck nodded.

Cavill lit a cigar and said, "Sergeant Major Welding, I seem to remember you saying your orders were to escort us across the desert."

"Correct," Welding said.

"We crossed the desert," Cavill said. "I suggest you return to your fort in the morning. From here on out, this is official police business."

"Jack is right," Duffy said. "Take your men back in the morning."

Welding nodded. "Agreed," he said.

■ ■ ■ ■

After breakfast, Duffy went to shake hands with Welding. "Well, Sergeant Major, thank you for the escort."

Welding shook Duffy's hand. "Goodluck, hope to see you again," Welding said.

"Safe travels back to the fort," Goodluck said.

"Buffalo Soldiers, mount," Welding said.

The six soldiers mounted their horses and with a nod, Welding led them back into the desert.

"All right, let's get moving," Duffy said.

Lopez led the way through the pass. Around noon, Duffy decided to stop and make camp.

"We can be through the pass in one hour," Lopez said. "We can make camp there."

"And walk into a sniper's bullet? No thanks," Duffy said. "Make camp. We'll leave after the moon is up."

After eating, they took naps with one man on guard duty per hour. Late in the afternoon, while Cavill was standing watch, he heard a horse walking through the pass.

"Jim," Cavill said. Duffy and Goodluck were instantly awake.

"Rider," Cavill said. "Just one."

Sato and Lopez got up, and the group waited for the lone rider to appear from around a bend.

It was Welding.

"Dammit, Sergeant, are you trying to get yourself killed?" Cavill said.

"Only since the day I was born," Welding said and dismounted. He looked at the coffeepot in the fire. "I could use a cup of that."

Goodluck filled a cup and handed it to Welding.

"Sergeant, what are you doing here?" Duffy said.

"I sent my men back and decided I'd lend you a hand," Welding said.

Duffy sighed.

"I'm here and I'm staying," Welding said. "Besides, I'm a civilian in a few weeks, and I don't cotton to sitting on my ass waiting for discharge."

"Let's fix some supper," Duffy said. "We leave after dark once the moon is up."

Goodluck led the group through the pass, guiding them by moonlight.

When he reached the end of the pass, he turned and rode back to the group.

"Lopez, from here, how far to Valdez's cabin?" Goodluck said.

"Maybe one thousand yards," Lopez said.

"You ride up front with me," Goodluck said.

Goodluck and Lopez pulled fifty feet ahead of the group, Goodluck expertly maneuvering the terrain by moonlight.

"He could track a mouse in a snowstorm," Welding said.

"If I know Joseph, he probably has," Duffy said.

Thirty minutes later, Goodluck and Lopez stopped and waited for the group to catch up.

"What is it?" Duffy said.

"Over this ridge is the hideout," Goodluck said. "We can walk up and take position."

Everybody dismounted. Goodluck, horse in tow, led the way up the ridge. Once everybody was on the ridge, they could see the faint outline of the cabin about one hundred yards below. Two lanterns illuminated the windows.

"All right, we have six hours to daylight. We might as well get some sleep," Duffy said. "I'll take first watch for one hour."

A few minutes before sunup, everybody was awake and eating a cold breakfast of jerky, cornbread, and water.

"We passed that water hole in the dark,"

Goodluck said. "We need to stop on the way out for water."

"Smoke from the chimney," Cavill said.

After a while, two men with rifles exited the cabin, went to the corral, and saddled their horses.

"Lookouts," Duffy said.

Once they saddled their horses, they left the corral and rode toward the pass.

"Joseph, can you take them quietly?" Duffy said.

Goodluck removed his bow and arrows from his saddle. He nodded and ran down the hill and out of sight.

"You're letting him go alone?" Weldon said.

"Don't worry about Joseph," Duffy said.

"Six horses left in the corral," Cavill said.

"Which they can't get to unless we let them," Duffy said.

"Lopez, do you know Valdez's horse?" Cavill said.

"The large pinto," Lopez said.

Duffy used the binoculars to look at the horses in the corral. "One pinto," he said.

"What do we do now?" Sato said.

"Wait for Joseph," Duffy said.

Cavill leaned against his saddle and lit a cigar. "We can't rush them. We'd be sitting ducks," he said. "They can't leave, or they'd be sitting ducks. I think you call this a Mexican standoff."

"We don't call it that," Lopez said. "We call it . . ."

"You shut up, or I'll have Joseph cut out your tongue," Cavill said.

"Where is Joseph?" Sato said. "Maybe I should go look for him?"

"I'm right here," Goodluck said as he returned to camp.

"Any trouble?" Duffy said.

"No," Goodluck said.

"We're studying on our next move," Cavill said. "We can't go down there, and they can't leave that cabin."

"Joseph, do you think you could hit the roof with an arrow from here?" Sato said.

Goodluck looked at the cabin. "Easily," he said.

"If we wrapped cloth around your arrow, poured whiskey on it, set it on fire, we could burn them out," Sato said. "Yes?"

"Yes," Duffy said. "Jack, get their attention."

Cavill stood, reached for his Winchester, and fired a shot through a window. The round echoed loudly for several seconds before fading away.

Duffy faced the cabin and cupped his hands. "King Valdez, this is the law," he

225

shouted. "The two riders you sent up to keep watch are dead. You can't get to your horses without us shooting you. Surrender now, and we'll let you live."

The cabin door opened and Valdez yelled, "Screw you, lawman."

"Jack," Duffy said.

Cavill fired six shots through the windows.

"You five men in there with Valdez, I'm going to give you something to think about," Duffy shouted. "We don't want you. We want Valdez. Give us Valdez and you go free. You have ten minutes to think it over."

While they waited, Goodluck made a fire and put on a pot of coffee.

"Hey, lawman," a man inside the cabin shouted.

"I'm here," Duffy shouted.

"We give you Valdez, you leave us alone?" the man shouted.

"You have my word," Duffy said.

"How can we trust you?" the man shouted.

"Joseph, put an arrow on the roof," Duffy said.

Goodluck fired an arrow high into the air and it landed on the roof.

"Hear that?" Duffy said. "That was an arrow. The next one will be on fire. We will burn you out and pick you off as you come out the front door. Now will you give us Valdez?"

"Yes, but how?" the man shouted.

"Tie him up and bring him out," Duffy shouted. "One of us will come get him. Any shooting and you burn. Agreed?"

"Agreed," the man shouted.

"A few minutes passed, the door opened, and Valdez, tied up with rope, was dragged out and tossed near the corral.

"Here is Valdez," a man shouted.

"Saddle his horse and we'll come get him," Duffy said.

"I'll go," Cavill said.

"Everybody be alert with your rifles. Joseph, keep that fire going," Duffy said.

Cavill mounted his horse. "Be right back," he said and galloped down the hill.

"The man has a set of stones on him like no tomorrow," Welding said.

"You don't know the half of it," Duffy said.

They watched as Cavill rode down the hill to flat ground and to the corral. He dismounted, grabbed Valdez, who was tied and gagged, and flung him over the saddle. Then he took the reins of Valdez's horse and galloped back up the hill.

At the camp, Cavill dismounted, grabbed Valdez, and tossed him to the ground. Cavill took his knife out of the sheath and cut the ropes binding Valdez's wrists and ankles. Valdez removed the gag from his mouth.

"You rotten pigs," Valdez said. "Cowards, all of you. Even my own men. Cowards."

Cavill grabbed Valdez by the throat and lifted him to his feet. In a show of strength, Cavill tightened his grip around Valdez's throat and actually lifted him off the ground.

"Jim," Goodluck said.

"Put him down, Jack," Duffy said.

Cavill looked at Duffy. "He killed Porter in cold blood," Cavill said.

"We need him alive," Duffy said. "Let him go."

Cavill released his grip and Valdez fell to the ground and gasped for air.

"You son of a bitch," Cavill said and walked away.

"Who wants coffee?" Goodluck said.

Valdez slowly stood up and looked at Lopez. "You sold my hide, you filthy Judas. God hates Judas and will punish you for this," Valdez said.

"Oh, be quiet, or I'll let Jack have his way with you," Duffy said.

Goodluck passed out cups of coffee to Duffy, Sato, and Welding.

"All right, Mr. Valdez, let's talk," Duffy said.

"Pour me some coffee to loosen my throat," Valdez said.

"That's our deal, Valdez," Duffy said. "One year or a noose. Take it or leave it. Either way, we are bringing you to Washington for prosecution."

Valdez looked at Lopez. "You give this Judas the same deal?" he said.

"Take it or leave it," Duffy said.

"I will take it because a year beats a noose," Valdez said. "But I want it in writing from your Justice Department, as you said."

"That's the deal," Duffy said. "Now if we are all in agreement, I'd like do some riding before dark."

"Go south and east and around the desert and then north to Tucson," Valdez said. "It will take only two and one half days."

"Joseph, find Jack, and let's get moving," Duffy said.

CHAPTER FORTY-FOUR

As supper cooked, Duffy studied his maps.

Valdez sipped coffee and looked at Goodluck. "It was you that killed my two men. How did you do it?"

"Bow and arrow," Goodluck said.

"Like the old days, eh, savage?" Valdez said. "Before the white man stripped you of your land, pride, and dignity."

"Is that why you kidnapped those children, to get back at the white man for the land you claim they stole?" Goodluck said.

"Claim?" Valdez said. "Texas was part of Mexico long before . . ."

"Valdez, shut up," Cavill said.

"And you," Valdez said as he looked at Welding. "Look at what the white man has done to your people."

Cavill drew his field knife. "I'm gonna cut your tongue out," he said.

"Jack, enough," Duffy said. "Valdez, be quiet, or I'm going to gag you."

Duffy ran his finger over the map. "Valdez, you've obviously come this way before. Where is the next water?" he said.

"Two hours' ride to the east," Valdez said.

Stirring the pans, Goodluck said, "Let's eat."

"Fill up the canteens. Let the horses drink and give them a short rest," Duffy said.

Cavill lit a cigar and Goodluck lit his pipe. "Jim, Jack, a moment," Goodluck said.

They walked away from the group to the shade of a tree.

"We're being dogged," Goodluck said.

"Are you sure?" Duffy said.

"I'm sure," Goodluck said.

"What do you think, Jack?" Duffy said.

"I've felt it myself," Cavill said. "I think Valdez cooked up a plan to surrender and then have his men dog us and kill us during the night."

"About how I see it," Goodluck said.

"How long before they catch us?" Duffy said.

"Before dark," Goodluck said. "Then they'll hang back and wait for us to go to sleep."

"Not if we get them first," Cavill said. "Joseph, you game?"

"Let's ride a bit and pick out a good

vantage point," Goodluck said.

Once the horses and mule were watered and rested, they rode for another hour until Goodluck spotted a hill that afforded the vantage point he wanted. Discreetly, Goodluck and Cavill hung back until the group was out of sight and then they rode up the hill.

After they secured the horses, they found good cover where they could see the five men pass.

"I got some jerky. What do you have?" Cavill said.

"Some cornbread and a few biscuits," Goodluck said.

"Bring a coffeepot?"

"I did."

"Let's get comfortable then."

"In the army we never leave a man behind," Welding said.

"We're not in the army, and Jack and Goodluck can take care of themselves," Duffy said.

"I've seen Mr. Cavill take on six men and walk away unscathed," Sato said.

"Maybe so, but I don't like it," Welding said.

"Relax, Sergeant Major," Duffy said. "We're just turning the tide on Mr. Valdez, is all. He set it up so his men would dog us in our sleep."

"Then we should have stayed and prepared for an attack," Welding said.

"Like I said, we're not in the army," Duffy said. "Our job is to protect and deliver the prisoners to Washington, to the Justice Department."

"I guess I have to get used to civilian ways," Welding said.

Duffy grinned. "If I had the slightest doubt about Jack and Goodluck's capabilities, we would have all stayed behind," he said. "Just like you do, I know my men."

Welding nodded. "In that regard, we're not much different," he said.

"Joseph, you make the best coffee," Cavill said as he dipped a biscuit into his cup.

"It's basically army coffee," Goodluck said. "One spoon for each cup and then one spoon extra."

Cavill ate the biscuit and washed it down with coffee. "How long you figure they're behind us?" he said.

"Two hours," Goodluck said.

Cavill took out a cigar and lit up.

Goodluck stuffed his pipe and leaned against his saddle. "We will have to kill them all," he said.

"I know," Cavill said.

Cavill rested against his saddle with his hat over his eyes.

"Jack," Goodluck said softly.

"I hear them," Cavill said. He removed his hat and sat up.

Goodluck put an arrow in his bow. Cavill cocked the lever of his Winchester.

"Take out the last two first," Cavill said. "I'll take the two in front."

They waited for the five riders to come into view. Then, in rapid succession, Goodluck put an arrow in the last two men, while Cavill took out the first two with his Winchester.

The fifth rider didn't move.

"In case you're wondering why you're still breathing, come up here and we'll tell you," Cavill shouted.

"Up there?" the man shouted.

"Or be shot atop that horse," Cavill said. "Which?"

The man shrugged. "I come up there," he said.

The man rode his horse up the hill where Cavill and Goodluck were standing. "Should I toss my gun?" he said.

"Keep it," Cavill said. "Go for it if you feel lucky."

"Nobody is that lucky," the man said.

"Step down and have a cup of coffee," Cavill said.

The man dismounted and Goodluck handed him a cup of coffee. "Thank you," the man said.

"What's your name?" Cavill said.

"Perez."

"Mexican?" Cavil said.

"I was born in Arizona," Perez said.

"How did you get mixed up with Valdez?" Cavill said.

"He is my third cousin," Perez said as he sipped coffee. "Very good coffee."

"The secret is to add one extra spoon," Cavill said. "What was your plan? To kill us all in our sleep?"

"If you wouldn't give him up peacefully," Perez said.

"As you have figured out by now, your plan was a failure," Cavill said.

"I agree. What now?" Perez said.

"That depends on if you want to live or not," Cavill said.

"Of course I want to live," Perez said.

"Give me your gun," Cavill said.

Perez flipped his Schofield to Cavill. "Nice-looking piece," he said. "Now we're going to ask some questions. If we don't like the answers, Joseph here is going to scalp you."

"What?" Perez said.

Goodluck drew his long, razor sharp field knife.

"First question," Cavill said, as he grabbed Perez by the shoulders and shoved him to his knees. "Is how long has Valdez had his little operation going?"

Goodluck grabbed Perez's hat from his head, tossed it aside, yanked his hair, and placed the knife against Perez's scalp.

"Mother of God," Perez said.

"Leave her out of this," Cavill said. "Answer the question."

"One year. About," Perez said.

"About?" Cavill said.

"Yes."

"How many kids have been stolen?" Cavill said.

"Three hundred, maybe more," Perez said.

"Good Lord," Cavill said. "How much money is involved?"

"I don't know."

"Joseph," Cavill said.

Goodluck yanked on Perez's hair and pressed the blade against Perez's scalp again.

"Wait. Stop. I'll tell you," Perez said. "He make thirty thousand a shipload."

"What does he pay you men?" Cavill said.

"A thousand a ship."

"A nice profit for himself," Cavill said. "Where does he keep his money?"

"He'll kill me I tell you that," Perez said.

"Joseph," Cavill said.

Goodluck drew a tiny drop of blood on Perez's scalp.

"Banco de Popular," Perez said.

Cavill nodded to Goodluck, and he lowered the knife.

"Stand up," Cavill said.

Perez stood.

"Get on your horse and start riding," Cavill said. "Don't stop until you reach California. Be grateful we don't kill you where you stand. Go."

Perez jumped on his horse. Cavill tossed him the Schofield.

"Adios," Cavill said.

Perez rode down the hill.

"Joseph, let's catch up to them before dark," Cavill said. "I'm hungry."

CHAPTER FORTY-FIVE

Cavill loaded a plate with beef, potatoes, carrots and beans, and a hunk of cornbread and sat against his saddle. "Where did you get the potatoes and carrots?" he said.

"Army issue," Welding said.

"I take it you had a good outcome," Duffy said.

On the opposite side of the fire, Valdez and Lopez sat together with their ankles shackled together.

Cavill looked at them.

"Your men are dead, Valdez," Cavill said. "Your little escape plan failed."

"One day I will kill you, big man," Valdez said.

"That will be the day," Cavill said.

"Valdez, it looks like you're going to have to keep our deal if you ever want to see the sunshine again," Duffy said.

"You killed all my men. You are a butcher," Valdez said. "Nothing but a vicious butcher."

"I can make it one more if you want me to," Cavill said.

"Valdez, shut up and eat your supper," Duffy said.

"Jim, we need to talk," Cavill said.

"Finish eating, and we'll take a stroll," Duffy said.

A bit later, Duffy, Cavill, Goodluck, Welding, and Sato took cups of coffee away from the fire to talk privately.

"We learned a few things from one of Valdez's men," Cavill said.

"I can imagine how you did that," Duffy said.

"Do you want the information or not?" Cavill said.

"Go ahead," Duffy said.

"The total number of missing kids is over three hundred," Cavill said.

"We suspected that," Duffy said.

"Valdez made thirty thousand a ship," Cavill said. "After paying his men, he banked twenty-five for himself. That's a lot of money. Maybe two hundred thousand or more."

"I'd like to know where he keeps it," Duffy said.

"Banco de Popular," Goodluck said.

Duffy looked at Goodluck.

"Exactly right," Cavill said.

"We'll keep that under wraps for now," Duffy said. "By the way, the one you got the information from, is he alive?"

"And in the wind," Cavill said.

"Let's get back, have a drink, and put the babies to bed," Duffy said.

After breakfast, they rode until noon, then took a break to rest the horses and mule for an hour.

Goodluck made a fire and put on a pot of coffee.

Duffy took out his maps.

"No need of a map," Welding said. "I know exactly where we are. We ride until dark, and then turn north to Tucson. Then it's two days' ride."

"You men are butchers," Valdez said. "You sold my hide, you filthy pigs. God will punish you for your crimes, you butcher."

"Do we have to listen to this all the way to Washington?" Cavill said.

"Valdez, one more word and you make the rest of the trip gagged," Duffy said. "Let's mount up."

Late in the afternoon, Duffy stopped the group when a large party of Navajo warriors came riding toward them from the north.

"Navajo hunting party," Welding said. "You men be quiet, especially you, Joseph Goodluck. That man in front is Cheveyo, the warrior and oldest son of the chief, and he does not like Comanche."

Welding rode toward the hunting party and stopped ten feet in front of Cheveyo.

"Sergeant Major Welding," Cheveyo said in English.

"Cheveyo, how do you fare these days?" Welding said.

"As they say in English, so-so," Cheveyo said. "Where are your troops?"

"This is a special detail," Welding said. "We are escorting prisoners to Tucson."

"That Comanche?" Cheveyo said.

"My prisoner and the two Mexicans," Welding said.

"Safe trip," Cheveyo said.

"And you," Welding said.

Cheveyo led his warriors past Welding and continued riding south.

Once they had passed, Welding turned his horse and rode back to the group.

"Let's go. We're wasting daylight," Welding said.

"I'll catch up with you," Goodluck said. "I'm going to hunt up some rabbits."

"Mind if I go with you?" Sato said.

"Let's go," Goodluck said.

After tying up the horses, Goodluck and Sato tracked several jackrabbits over some hills.

Goodluck took his bow and arrows.

Sato carried a small, leather pouch over his left shoulder.

They stopped within one hundred feet of a large jackrabbit. His bow at the ready, Goodluck took aim and felled the rabbit before it could move.

"We need at least three more," Goodluck said.

"The next one is mine," Sato said.

"Can you use a bow?" Goodluck said.

Sato removed a Bo-shuriken from the pouch. "We call it a throwing star," he said.

They tracked a second jackrabbit sitting beside its lair. Sato aimed the throwing star and brought the rabbit down with a perfect throw.

"Two more should do it," Goodluck said.

Forty pounds of jackrabbit made a fine, large stew.

"Good hunting, Joseph," Duffy said.

"I only got one," Goodluck said. "Sato got three."

"You can use a bow?" Duffy said.

"Show him," Goodluck said.

"With this," Sato said and removed his throwing star from the pouch.

"What is that?" Cavill said.

"Bo-shuriken," Sato said. "A throwing star."

Sato passed the Bo-shuriken to Duffy.

"Razor sharp," Duffy said. "When there is time, maybe you could teach us how to use it."

"I would be happy to," Sato said.

"Is there enough for seconds?" Cavill said.

CHAPTER FORTY-SIX

Welding led the way into Tucson. It was a large town of eight thousand and well known for being a wild cowboy town.

It was at the train station where Wyatt Earp killed Frank Stilwell, who was waiting to ambush Wyatt's brother Virgil.

"Who is sheriff in Tucson, do you know?" Duffy said to Welding.

"Bob Pearl," Welding said. "Used to be a Wells Fargo agent."

"Let's go see the man," Duffy said.

They rode to the center of town where the sheriff's office was located on Main Street.

Sheriff Bob Pearl was behind his desk and smiled at Welding.

"I didn't know the army was in town, Titus," Pearl said.

"It's not. I'm working with these fellows on a separate issue," Welding said. "And we'd like to keep two prisoners overnight."

"Bring them in, go get settled, and tell me about it over dinner," Pearl said.

The largest hotel in town was the Hotel Tucson. It had its own livery, telegraph, barbershop, and a bathing room with six tubs.

Except for Goodluck and Sato, the group visited the barber for a shave before soaking in a hot tub. They left their dirty clothes for laundering.

Cavill, Duffy, and Welding smoked cigars as they soaked in the hot water. Goodluck smoked his pipe.

"Sergeant Major, I have a proposal for you," Duffy said. "When you leave the army, come to our office in Springfield. I'd like to offer you a position as one of our agents."

"That's a fine idea," Cavill said. "Especially since we're planning on expanding to California."

"California?" Welding said.

"Sacramento," Duffy said.

"Two questions," Welding said. "What does an agent do, and what does the job pay?"

"We are licensed private detectives as well as federal constables," Duffy said. "Our agency is hired for many reasons. We solve crimes, make arrests, and in some cases work directly for the Justice Department. We use a lot of forensic science in our work as well."

"I won't pretend to know what that is," Welding said.

"That's teachable," Duffy said. "Your experience isn't. As for your second question, a great deal more money than the army pays."

"When do you get out?" Cavill said.

"Two weeks," Welding said.

"Come see us," Duffy said. "On your way to Boston. We could use an old Buffalo Soldier."

"This steak is perfect," Cavill said.

"You're in cattle country," Pearl said.

"Anyway, that's our reason for borrowing your jail," Duffy said.

"It's a pretty good reason," Pearl said. "I read some telegram notices on King Valdez, but I never knew he was in Arizona."

"After tomorrow he won't be," Duffy said.

"How about a drink after dinner?" Pearl said. "We have an ordinance against wearing firearms in the town limits, but it doesn't apply to peace officers."

The Bucket of Blood Saloon was the largest saloon in Tucson, with a bar that extended one hundred feet. There were six gambling tables, including a roulette wheel.

A piano player played lively background music. Twenty of twenty-four tables were occupied.

Pearl led them to one of the four empty tables.

"I'll get us a bottle and glasses," Cavill said. He went to the bar and ordered a bottle of bourbon and six glasses. The bartender placed them on a tray and Cavill headed back to the table.

As Cavill passed a table where six men were playing cards, one said, "An Indian, a Chinaman, and now a stinking darkie. I guess they let anybody in here these days."

Without breaking stride, holding the tray in his left hand, Cavill drew his Colt with his right hand and smacked the man across the skull, knocking him unconscious to the floor.

Cavill holstered his Colt, set the tray on the table, and took his chair.

Duffy reached for the bottle and poured drinks.

"Hey, Sheriff," a man at the table where the unconscious player had been seated said. "Are you going to do something about this?"

"About what?" Pearl said.

"What that big ape did to our friend," the man said.

"Why don't you come over here and do something about it yourself?" Pearl said.

The man said, "Come on, boys, let's get him out of here."

"Sheriff, to your good health," Duffy said and raised his glass.

CHAPTER FORTY-SEVEN

At the train station, Welding shook hands with the group.

"We'll be expecting you in three weeks or so," Duffy said.

"I'll be there," Welding said.

"Hey, Jim, what did you do with the mule?" Cavill said.

"Sold it for twenty five dollars to the livery," Duffy said.

As they entered the train, Cavill said, "Another forty-eight hours on a train."

The train had a prisoner car with two cells. Once Valdez and Lopez were locked safely away in separate cells, the group went to breakfast in the dining car.

"Do you think Welding will show up?" Cavill said.

"I do," Duffy said. "He's a good man. I'd like to have him."

"Have you heard from Miss Potts?"

Cavill said.

"Not since we've been on the trail," Duffy said. "I wired her this morning and also Poule in Washington."

"Any news from Kathy?" Cavill said.

"No. Any from Joey?"

"Nope."

"We certainly have a way for losing women, don't we?"

"Yup."

While Quill and Harvey continued Porter's work on compiling a mug book to take to Washington, Holt tested various powders and inks for fingerprinting.

Miss Potts returned from the post office with a stack of mail. She filled a mug with coffee from the pot keeping warm on the stove and went to her office.

Holt came into her office. "I think there is one powder that works best above the others," he said.

"Can you field-test it before Jim takes it to the Justice Department?" Miss Potts said.

"I can. Where are those fingerprint cards Charles was designing?" Holt said.

Miss Potts opened a desk drawer, removed a stack of cards, and handed them to Holt.

"I'll start right here with us," Holt said. "Let me get the ink and pad."

Holt left the office and returned a moment later with a pad, bottle of ink, and a small roller. He set them on the table beside Miss Potts's desk.

"Ink," Holt said and poured a bit on the pad and then used the roller to spread it evenly.

"Thumb," Holt said and took hold of Miss Potts's right hand. He looked at her hand and grinned. "This sets a man's mind to thinking," he said.

"Never mind your thinking," Miss Potts said. "Keep your mind on your work, and we can discuss your thinking later."

Holt took Miss Potts's thumbprint and then his own. After that, he took Quill and Harvey's.

"Charles was on to something with this," Holt said.

"With these mug books as well," Quill said.

"He was a thinking man and ahead of his time," Harvey said. "That's for sure."

Miss Potts walked into the work area holding a telegram. "Jim and the others are on a train to Washington, arriving in two days."

"From where?" Holt said.

"Arizona," Miss Potts said.

"Maybe we should meet him there?" Quill said.

"If Jim needs you, he'll send for you," Miss Potts said.

She returned to her office, sat at her desk, and sorted through the mail. Mixed in with the regular bills, payments, and requests were two letters. One from Joey Jordan and one from Kathy Bodine.

Instinctively, she knew the news wasn't good. She knew both communications were goodbye letters.

Kathy, if she was returning, would have returned by now.

And Joey Jordan just got tired of waiting and dealing with broken promises.

Who could blame them?

"Lester, could you come in here for a moment," Miss Potts said.

Holt entered the office.

"Close the door and then kiss me," Miss Potts said.

CHAPTER FORTY-EIGHT

Poule and two US Marshals met them at the train station.

"Good to see you again, Jim," Poule said. "I hope you don't hold sending the army against me."

"They came in handy crossing the desert," Duffy said.

"The marshals will hold Valdez and the other one in custody until we need them," Poule said. "Shall we go to the office?"

"I think we'd rather go to lunch first and check into the hotel," Duffy said.

"Of course," Poule said. "Stop by the office when you're ready."

After checking into the hotel and boarding the horses, the men grabbed a hot bath, a change of clothes, and met in the hotel dining room for lunch.

After lunch, Duffy used the hotel telegraph to send a wire to Miss Potts. Then they walked to the Justice Department to meet Poule.

"This time tomorrow Lopez will be on his way to Folsom to serve eleven months," Poule said.

"Where is Valdez?" Duffy said.

"In the holding room with the marshals," Poule said.

"Before you bring him in, we have some new developments," Duffy said.

"Oh?" Poule said.

"We have it from one of his men that the total number of missing children exceeds three hundred," Duffy said. "Also we discovered Valdez makes about twenty-five thousand for each shipment of children, and he keeps his money in *Banco de Popular* in Mexico."

"I will ask the Mexican authorities to seize his assets," Poule said.

"We figured you'd do that," Duffy said. "But don't let on to Valdez that we know anything about the money. He'll be more inclined to deal if he thinks he's coming out after a year as a rich man."

Poule nodded. "I believe you are right," he said.

"Let's get him in here," Duffy said.

"Where are your people? Do you want them to sit in with us?" Poule said.

"I think they've had enough of him," Duffy said. "I know Jack has."

Poule went to the door and opened it. "Bring in Valdez," he said to a marshal waiting in the hall.

Poule went to the ceramic coffeepot on the table and filled three cups. "Still hot," he said and took his chair.

Two marshals escorted Valdez into the room. Valdez's wrists and ankles were shackled.

"Have a seat," Poule said.

"Want us to stay?" a marshal said.

"No, thank you," Poule said.

After the marshals left the office and closed the door, Poule took a sip of coffee. "It's good. Help yourself," he said.

Valdez needed to use two hands to lift the cup and sip.

"Here is my offer and it's nonnegotiable," Poule said.

"What does that mean non . . . ?" Valdez said.

"It mean there's no arguing the point," Poule said. "I make the offer, and you accept or decline. Understand?"

"I understand," Valdez said.

"Okay. Here is my offer," Poule said. "One year in a federal prison in exchange for the man you work for and where we can find him. If you refuse, you will hang, or at best spend the rest of your life at hard labor."

"I do one year and I'm free?" Valdez said.

"One year."

"You put that in writing?"

"Of course," Poule said. "It isn't binding unless it's in writing."

"If you think I want to hang or spend the next forty years in prison, then you know nothing about King Valdez," Valdez said.

"Then you agree to our deal?"

"Yes. But in writing first," Valdez said.

Poule opened a file on the desk, removed a legal document, and slid it across to Valdez. "Do you read English?" Poule said.

"I read English very well," Valdez said.

"Read it," Poule said.

Valdez picked up the two-page legal document and read it carefully. When he was done, he lowered the papers.

"Questions?" Poule said.

"Where is Lopez going?" Valdez said.

"Folsom Prison," Poule said.

"I would like to go there as well."

"So you can kill him?" Poule said. "Nice try, but no. Any more questions?"

"What does time served against time spent in transit mean?" Valdez said.

"It means time reduced for your services," Poule said. "Now, where is your contact man and what is his name?"

"His name is Bill Maddux," Valdez said. "Before your Civil War he was a slave trader out of Georgia. He became very rich peddling flesh. He disappeared, knowing he would be arrested if the south lost. The south lost."

"Go on," Poule said.

"I met him a few years back when I was dealing in guns on the black market," Valdez said. "He was a supplier. He was in Mexico selling guns to the revolutionaries. He told me he had a more lucrative way of making money if I was interested. I was interested."

"Selling children?" Poule said.

"I sell nothing. I supply the children. Maddux sells them," Valdez said.

"How are arrangements made?" Poule said.

"He sends me a telegram with dates and times his privateer ships will be in port, what ports, and for how long," Valdez said. "I deliver the children, and the captain of the privateer ship pays me."

"Where do you receive the telegram?" Poule said.

"Tucson."

"Is there one there now?" Poule said.

"I do not know. I am here, not there."

257

Poule scribbled a note, then took it to the door, opened it, and said, "Marshal, would you take this to our telegraph operator and wait for a reply."

Poule handed the note to the marshal, closed the door, and took his seat.

"Where does Maddux live?" Poule said.

"Canada."

"Canada? Canada is a big country. Where in Canada?" Poule said.

"That I do not know," Valdez said.

"I'm afraid that's not good enough," Duffy said. "We need Maddux, or there's no deal."

"Like you said, Canada is a big country," Valdez said. "How am I supposed to know where he lives?"

"You're going to help us find him, or it's a noose for you," Duffy said. "Understand?"

"Like I said, if you think I want to hang by the neck until dead, you don't know King Valdez," Valdez said.

"That's good, because if you don't want your neck stretched like an ostrich, you'll do everything you can to help us find Maddux," Duffy said. "Right?"

Valdez nodded.

"Good," Duffy said.

"That's all for now," Poule said. "I'll have a marshal take you back to your cell."

■ ■ ■ ■

At the conference table in his office, Poule explained the situation to Cavill, Goodluck, and Sato.

"I should have killed the son of a bitch when I had the chance," Cavill said.

"That son of a bitch is going to help us get a war criminal and slave trader," Duffy said.

There was a knock on the door.

"Enter," Poule said.

The door opened and a marshal stepped in and handed Poule a telegram. "From Tucson, sir," the marshal said.

"Wait outside," Poule said.

The marshal left the office and closed the door.

Poule read the telegram and handed it to Duffy. "Maddux will have privateer ships in Baltimore and Miami on the first and fifth of September," Duffy said after reading the text. "We need to know the origin of the telegram."

Poule went to the door again, opened it, and said, "Marshal, wire Tucson and ask for the origin of the telegram."

For twenty minutes they sat around drinking coffee and wondering. The answer came when the marshal knocked on the door.

"Enter," Poule said.

The marshal opened the door, stepped inside, and said, "Montreal."

Chapter Forty-Nine

"Our first order of business is to respond to Maddux's telegram and let him know Valdez will be ready on September first and fifth," Poule said.

They were having dinner at a restaurant in the section of Washington known as Capitol Hill.

The restaurant was elite and crowded with senators, congressmen, and lobbyists.

"The response needs to come from Tucson," Duffy said. "In the morning, we'll send a wire to Sheriff Pearl in Tucson and ask for his help. He can send the telegram for us to Maddux, so it won't appear suspicious."

"Since Valdez doesn't set foot in Tucson, he must have one of his men do the sending and receiving," Cavill said.

"Maddux will have no way of knowing it was us that sent the wire," Poule said.

"Don't be so sure," Duffy said. "There

261

might be some kind of code involved."

"We'll talk to Valdez in the morning and find out," Poule said.

"Why do you suppose he chose Montreal?" Sato said.

"It's very close to America. They speak French and English in Montreal," Duffy said. "And he probably speaks French."

"Joseph speaks French," Cavill said.

"And Spanish," Goodluck said.

"Tom, can you get us into Canada?" Duffy said.

"Now hold on, Jim," Poule said. "We'll let the Mounties handle . . ."

"The hell we will," Cavill snapped. "We didn't have our boss murdered and track this asshole through a desert just to hand the whole thing over to some Canadian Mounties. No way in hell that happens."

"I agree with Jack," Goodluck said.

"As do I," Sato said.

Poule looked at Duffy. "Jim?"

"I have to go along with the boys, Tom," Duffy said. "Maddux is ours. We earned the right."

"It's a lot of paperwork," Poule said.

"Hang the paperwork," Cavill said. "Or I'll sneak into Canada and go after the bastard alone."

"He will, Tom," Duffy said. "Believe me."

Poule sighed. "I'll do the paperwork, but it's more than likely you'll have to work with the Mounties."

"I'll work with Satan himself to catch this bastard," Cavill said.

"First things first," Poule said. "We speak to Valdez in the morning and then send a telegram. Then we do our homework."

"We have five weeks until September first," Duffy said. "We need to know everything about Maddux, including his shoe size and favorite dessert."

While Goodluck and Sato played chess in the lobby of the hotel, Cavill and Duffy sat outside on the porch. Each had a small glass of whiskey and a cigar.

"I'd have to say at this point that if Kathy was coming back, she would have by now," Duffy said.

"What do you think happened?" Cavill said.

"She got back to Fort Jones and discovered they needed her more than she needed Springfield," Duffy said.

"I suppose there is no way you could run the agency from Fort Jones?" Cavill said.

"Hardly," Duffy said. "Remember the place. It's three days' ride to a telegraph line."

Cavill nodded. "I can't say as I blame Joey for dumping me," he said. "I saddled her with two kids and told her I'd be right back. Six months later, I'm not back."

"Maybe Charles Porter was right about no married men?" Duffy said.

"Maybe?" Cavill said.

"The job and marriage don't seem to go together," Duffy said.

"There are plenty of lawmen with wives and families," Cavill said. "Maybe it's us."

"Kathy is not going to quit being a doctor, and Joey isn't giving up her ranch, so maybe you're right," Duffy said.

"I hate being right," Cavill said. "Being right doesn't keep me warm at night."

"Maybe another drink will?" Duffy said.

"There isn't enough whiskey in the whole damn country that could take the place of Joey," Cavill said as he stood up. "But I'm willing to try."

Duffy stood and said, "This round is on me."

CHAPTER FIFTY

"You're going to buy us some time, Mr. Valdez," Poule said and showed Valdez the telegram from Maddux.

Valdez read it quickly and said, "The first and fifth of September. That's in five weeks."

"And you're going to agree to deliver children to him on those days," Poule said. "We will respond to Maddux. What we need to know is how you normally respond."

"How?" Valdez said.

"Obviously, you must communicate in some sort of code," Duffy said. "How would you respond to let Maddux know you agree to his request?"

"Simple," Valdez said. "Have you pencil and paper?"

Poule slid paper and pencil across the table to Valdez. Valdez picked up the pencil and wrote a quick telegram and then slid the paper back to Poule.

"Shipment will be ready on the 1st and

5th. KV," Poule read.

"Like I said, simple," Valdez said.

"His telegram came out of Montreal," Poule said. "We know from the telegraph code. What we don't know is: did he send it himself, have someone send it for him, or if he's even in Montreal."

"He is a very careful man," Valdez said. "He would not go himself to send a telegram. He would send one of his men."

"We thought not," Poule said. "After you agree to deliver the children, would you send another telegram to Maddux?"

"Two days before delivery, I would send another telegram telling him everything is ready," Valdez said.

"All right. That's all for now," Poule said.

Poule took Duffy, Cavill, Goodluck, and Sato to lunch at a restaurant on the Hill.

"By now Sheriff Pearl has sent the response to Maddux, so we have a little more than a month to work with," Poule said.

"Maddux must be pretty confident to risk two more privateer ships so soon after he just lost two," Duffy said. "My guess is he doesn't know we have Valdez, and losing a few ships is the cost of doing business."

"That's all well and good, but how do we find him?" Poule said.

"The first thing we have to do is our homework," Duffy said.

"I knew you were going to say that," Cavill said. "Can it wait until after dessert?"

In the Justice Department records room, Duffy and Poule searched old records of war criminals from the Civil War.

Bill Maddux was listed as "missing."

His biography, however, was extensive. He was born fifty-five years ago in Toronto, Canada, to a French family. When he was ten years old, the family purchased a large cotton plantation in Georgia. Along with the plantation came two hundred slaves.

By the time he was fifteen, Maddux had learned the business of slavery so well, his father trusted him enough to allow him to buy slaves at the auction houses in Atlanta.

When he was twenty, after recognizing the vast amount of money to be made in the slave-trading business, Maddux left the plantation and became a full-time trader.

For the next decade, Maddux made connections all over the world, became a top slave trader, and made a fortune in the process. He bought and sold slaves in other countries besides America, including Cuba, many islands in the Caribbean, Europe, and the Far East.

Before the first shot was fired in the first battle of the Civil War, Maddux vanished without a trace.

His family lost everything to the war. The plantation, their fortune, and finally their lives.

A war crimes commission searched for Maddux for many years before closing the file on him. What family he had remaining in Toronto claimed they knew nothing of his whereabouts.

"So he disappears for two decades and resurfaces a year ago, back in business," Duffy said. "Why?"

"The obvious answer is he lost his fortune," Poule said.

"Right. So he looks up old contacts in the black market, makes some new ones, and is back in business," Duffy said.

"I'm afraid the demand for male child labor and young female sex slaves is very high in certain parts of the world," Poule said.

Duffy sighed. "Yeah," he said. "And somebody somewhere knows where Maddux is hiding."

"Yes, but who?" Poule said.

CHAPTER FIFTY-ONE

"Valdez said he gets paid by the privateer ship's captains," Duffy said.

"That means the captains deal with somebody close to Maddux," Cavill said.

"Tom, where are those captains right now?" Duffy said.

"I had them extradited to Washington," Poule said. "They should be here some time tomorrow morning."

"If we offer them a deal for information, they should give us what we want in exchange," Duffy said.

The group was having dinner at the hotel. A clerk from the desk approached the table with a telegram and handed it to Duffy.

"Thank you," Duffy said. He opened the telegram and read it quickly. "It's from Miss Potts. She has assignments for the men and wants to know if she should take them."

"What kind of assignments?" Cavill said.

"She doesn't say," Duffy said. "I'll reply

and ask for specifics."

"It's six o'clock. Shouldn't we lock up and get going?" Holt said.

"Lester, don't be so impatient," Miss Potts said.

"We've been cooped up in this . . ." Holt said just as the telegraph on Miss Potts's desk clicked.

Miss Potts grabbed a pencil and wrote down the message on a pad. "It's from Jim," she said. "He wants to know about the cases I wired him about."

Duffy and Cavill waited on the sofa in the hotel lobby. Each had a drink and a cigar. Goodluck and Sato were engaged in a game of chess at a table nearby.

"If we can get the privateer ships' captains to turn, we'll know where the money comes from," Duffy said.

"They'll turn when Poule offers them the same deal he offered Valdez," Cavill said.

A desk clerk approached Duffy and Cavill with a telegram. "Just came in," the clerk said and handed the telegram to Duffy.

Duffy read it and said, "Miss Potts has two cases that need our attention."

"To tell you the truth, Jim, I'm sick of sitting around hotel rooms," Cavill said.

"Joseph and Sato feel the same."

Miss Potts waited at her desk. Lester came up behind her and nibbled on her neck.

"Lester, please," Miss Potts said.

"I aim to," Holt said.

The telegraph clicked and Miss Potts grabbed a pencil. After she finished writing the message, she said, "Joseph, Jack, and Mr. Sato will be here in two days."

"Now can we go?" Holt said.

"Yes, Lester, now we can go," Miss Potts said.

Duffy, Cavill, Goodluck, and Sato sat at the hotel bar with glasses of whiskey.

"I'm just grateful for something to do," Cavill said.

"Hotel rooms do get boring," Goodluck said.

"You should be able to wrap things up in two weeks," Duffy said. "After that, no more assignments until we know what we're doing with Maddux."

"What about Titus Welding?" Cavill said. "He should be in Springfield by the time we finish these new assignments."

"That's right," Duffy said. "I'll send Miss Potts a telegram about him in the morning."

"Well, Joseph, how about another game of chess?" Sato said.

"Why not?" Goodluck said.

Goodluck and Sato left the bar.

"We could watch the game," Duffy said.

"We could," Cavill said. "After another round of drinks."

Chapter Fifty-Two

After breakfast, Cavill, Goodluck, and Sato walked their horses to the train station, while Duffy walked to the Justice Department.

Poule was at his desk when Duffy arrived at his office.

"The train arrived at ten this morning," Poule said. "Marshals will escort the two ships' captains here for interrogation."

"This better work," Duffy said. "We'd better catch Maddux, or we're giving the store away to men who should be hanged or in prison for life."

"I know how you feel," Poule said. "Let's get some coffee and wait in the interrogation room."

"The United States Marshal in Cheyenne, Wyoming, has some doubts about a man convicted of murder," Miss Potts said. "He heard about our ballistic testing and asked

273

us for help."

"What's the other assignment?" Quill said.

"Do you remember Police Chief Coffey in Seattle?" Miss Potts said.

"Of course," Quill said.

"They arrested a man suspected of murder," Miss Potts said. "The suspect beat a man to death with a club. The man claims he's innocent, and Coffey thinks he just might be. He heard about our testing with fingerprints and wants to give it a try."

"We know Coffey," Harvey said. "We'll take this case."

"Pack what you need and take the morning train west," Miss Potts said. "I'll wire Coffey and let him know you're coming."

"What about me?" Holt said.

"I need you here until the others arrive from Washington," Miss Potts said.

Poule and Duffy sat opposite the captain of the privateer ship confiscated in Portland.

"I assume there is no need to tell you that you are in a great deal of trouble," Poule said.

"No shit," the captain said.

"At best you're looking at twenty years," Poule said. "At worst, you'll be hung."

"Hung? I killed nobody," the captain said.

"You were caught smuggling children out

of the country for the purpose of slavery," Poule said. "You'll be hung."

"Unless?" the captain said.

"You tell us what we want to know," Poule said.

"What do you want to know?" the captain said.

"Let's start with Maddux," Poule said.

"Who?" the captain said.

"He's the man you work for," Poule said.

"As far as I know, I was hired by a man named King Valdez," the captain said.

"The noose is getting tighter by the minute," Poule said.

"It's true. I wouldn't lie to protect someone I never heard of," the captain said. "As far as I know, I was hired by King Valdez."

"How were you paid?" Duffy said. "We know the captain of each privateer ship paid Valdez, so who paid you?"

"That is something entirely different," the captain said. "The night before the children are delivered, a man arrives with thirty thousand for Valdez and the like amount for me and my crew."

"A man?" Duffy said.

"Yes, a man. He never tells me his name or who he works for, and I don't ask," the captain said. "He says the money is for me and Valdez. That's all I know. I swear it."

"We'll get back to you," Poule said.

"A man shows up at the pier or in a bar and says he wants to hire my ship," the captain arrested in Portland said. "He says I can make thirty thousand for a few weeks' work. He says the man I will work for is King Valdez."

"And you never heard of Maddux?" Duffy said.

"Not before this very moment," the captain said. "I have no wish to be hung. Why would I lie to you?"

"To keep from being hung," Duffy said.

"But I am speaking true to you," the captain said.

"How do you get paid?" Duffy said.

"One or two nights before Valdez delivers the children, a man arrives with money," the captain said. "He doesn't say his name, and I don't ask."

"How much?" Duffy said.

"Sixty thousand," the captain said. "Half for me, half for Valdez."

"We'll get back to you," Poule said.

"Wait, what about my deal?" the captain said.

"What are you thinking?" Poule said.

In Poule's office, Duffy sipped coffee and

smoked a cigar from the sofa.

"I'm thinking we could use one of these idiots to our advantage," Duffy said.

"How?" Poule said.

"We confiscated their ships," Duffy said. "Maddux's man is expecting a ship and a captain. One in Miami and one in Baltimore. We just so happen to have a ship and a captain for each."

Poule nodded and then grinned. "What a coincidence," he said.

CHAPTER FIFTY-THREE

In Poule's office, Poule and Duffy sat at the conference table. Each had a cup of coffee. A ceramic pot rested between them.

"If we can catch the man delivering the money to the captain, he can lead us to Maddux," Duffy said.

"We only have one shot at this. On the first," Poule said. "If we screw it up there will be no man with money on the fifth."

"So let's not screw it up," Duffy said.

"Which captain should we pick?" Poule said.

"Both," Duffy said. "A week before the first, Maddux is bound to have both piers watched."

Poule nodded. "Both it is," he said. "Let's go see the captains."

The two captains sat across the table from Poule and Duffy in the interrogation room.

"Here is my offer," Poule said. "You do

exactly as I say to the letter, and you both get off with one year in prison. Otherwise you face twenty years to life."

"I am not a stupid man," a captain said.

"Nor I," the other captain said. "What do you want us to do?"

"Help us catch Maddux, and you both do one, easy year," Poule said.

"You put that in writing?" a captain said.

"Guaranteed," Poule said.

"How can we help you catch Maddux?" the other captain said.

Duffy and Poule sat across the desk of the admiral of the Coast Guard.

"I have to admit that is quite the scheme you just presented me," the admiral said.

"It's our only chance at capturing not only a slaver and war criminal, but a kidnapper and child slaver," Duffy said.

"When do you want those ships in the harbors?" the admiral said.

"August thirtieth and September second should do," Duffy said.

"They will be there and so will a dozen Coast Guard to act as crew," the admiral said.

"Thank you, Admiral," Poule said.

Poule and Duffy sat opposite the two captains in the interrogation room.

"So you're going to get your one chance at one year in prison instead of life," Poule said. "But you have to do exactly as we say to the letter. Any slipups, no matter whose fault it is, and you do life. Am I understood?"

"Perfectly," a captain said.

"Yes," the other captain said.

"Here is the deal," Poule said. "Your ships will be delivered to Baltimore and Miami before the first and fifth of September. Your crew will be made up of US Marshals and Coast Guard. When the man comes to deliver the money he will be apprehended and then our deal begins. Agreed?"

"Yes," a captain said.

"Agreed," the other captain said.

At dinner in the hotel dining room, Duffy and Poule cut into steaks.

"We can work out the details over the next few days. Then I think I can return to the office for a few weeks," Duffy said. "I'll be back around the twenty-fifth or so with my men."

"Do we need them?" Poule said. "We have enough manpower between the Coast Guard and marshals to do the job."

"We started this investigation months ago

with just one missing child," Duffy said. "My people have earned the right to finish this, wherever it goes."

Poule nodded. "On one condition," he said.

"What's that?" Duffy said.

"You consider my job offer," Poule said. "Justice needs men like you, Jim."

"When this is over, I'll consider it," Duffy said.

"Good enough," Poule said.

CHAPTER FIFTY-FOUR

Goodluck, Cavill, and Sato rode their horses from the railroad station in Springfield to the office and put the horses in the company livery.

Miss Potts was in the office when they walked in. She jumped up from her desk to greet them warmly.

"You men look worn out from the train journey," Miss Potts said. "Go home and get cleaned up, and we'll go to lunch. I'll fill you in on what's going on around here."

"Quill and Harvey?" Cavill said.

"Should be in Seattle late this afternoon," Miss Potts said.

"And Holt?" Cavill said.

"Went for the mail."

"Quill and Harvey are going to help with a murder investigation in Seattle where finger-prints might be useful," Miss Potts said.

"And what do you have for us?"

Cavill said.

"The marshal in Cheyenne has some doubt about a murder and wants you to do some ballistic testing for him," Miss Potts said.

"I haven't been to Cheyenne since last year," Cavill said.

"We'll pick up tickets on the way back to the office," Miss Potts said. "How are things in Washington?"

Cavill and Goodluck filled Miss Potts in on the progress in Washington while they ate lunch.

"I received a telegram from Jim this morning," Miss Potts said. "He's coming home for a few weeks."

"I imagine he got everything in place for September first, so a few weeks of rest will do him good," Cavill said.

"Mr. Sato, do you want to go to Cheyenne with Jack and Joseph?" Miss Potts said.

"Very much," Sato said. "It's part of my education."

"I realize you men want to go home and get some rest before tomorrow, but, Jack, could you come back with me to the office for a moment?" Miss Potts said.

"Of course," Cavill said.

Miss Potts handed Cavill the letter from

Joey Jordan.

"I was expecting it," Cavill said. "I'll read it at home."

Cavill walked home from the office, a distance of less than a mile. Sato was in his room, probably asleep, when Cavill went to the den and poured a drink of whiskey. He sat in the leather chair beside a small table and lit a cigar.

Then he opened the letter and read.

The news was as expected.

Joey was cutting him loose. He read the letter twice and then laid it on the table.

Sato entered the room. "I heard you come in," he said. He looked at the letter on the table. "Bad news?"

"My girl Joey," Cavill said. "She broke it off. I can't say it wasn't expected."

"I am sorry," Sato said.

"I don't blame her," Cavill said. "Joey is a wonderful woman with a heart as big as her ranch. She took in the two orphans I dumped at her doorstep and made them her own. The problem is me. I'm just not cut out to be a full-time cowboy. That's what it would mean if I stayed."

"Jack, we are what we are," Sato said. "All of us."

"I expect so," Cavill said.

■ ■ ■ ■

Before they went to sleep, Miss Potts and Holt had a small glass of brandy in Holt's study.

"I'm afraid when Jim arrives and we tell him we wish to be married, he may be against the idea," Miss Potts said.

"In that case, I'm prepared to quit the agency," Holt said. "We both have a house and a fair amount in the bank. We can do what we want."

"Can we have a real honeymoon?" Miss Potts said.

"Sure," Holt said. "Anywhere you want."

"Let's go to bed," Miss Potts said.

CHAPTER FIFTY-FIVE

"His name is Judd Thornton," Chief Coffey said. "Two days ago, or rather nights ago, he was drinking and playing cards in the Golden Eagle Saloon near the waterfront. He's a logger, and with some friends was letting off some steam. He got into an argument with the victim over a pot, and it lead to a fight."

"In the saloon?" Quill said.

"Yes, and the saloon bouncers broke it up, but not before threats were made by both parties," Coffey said. "Firearms aren't permitted inside the town limits, but knives and other types of weapons are. The victim was found beaten to death in an alleyway in the morning. Two of my officers went to Thornton's hotel room and found him drunk and with a billy club in his possession."

"And he claimed innocence?" Harvey said.

"Yes, and frankly, in the condition he was

in, I don't see how he even made it to his hotel room, much less beat a man to death," Coffey said.

"Where is the club?" Quill said.

"Locked up," Coffey said.

"Put on some gloves and get it," Harvey said.

After dusting the billy club carefully, Quill and Harvey inspected every square inch of it with a powerful magnifying glass.

Coffey, fascinated, watched the entire process.

"We have a perfect set of thumbprints on the club," Quill said.

"We'd like to compare them to Thornton's," Harvey said.

Thornton didn't quite understand what was happening, but he allowed Quill and Harvey to take prints of both of his thumbs.

Coffey watched the process of inking Thornton's thumbs and transferring the prints to a card.

They returned to Coffey's office where the prints on the card were compared to the prints on the billy club.

"They aren't even close," Quill said.

"He's not your man," Harvey said.

"We need to convince the prosecutor,"

Coffey said.

"You boys are staying overnight?" Coffey said.

"As long as it takes," Quill said.

"We'll see the prosecutor in the morning," Coffey said.

At their hotel, Quill and Harvey sent a wire to Miss Potts and then went to have an early dinner in the dining room.

"If we convince the prosecutor Thornton is innocent, that leaves Coffey without a suspect," Quill said.

"True, but that's not what we were hired for," Harvey said.

"True, but we have a little time before we need to return to the office, so why not stay and see if we can be of some help?" Quill said.

"Since Coffey is paying our fee, it should be his decision," Harvey said.

"We'll ask him in the morning," Quill said.

"Agreed."

After breakfast, Quill, Harvey, and Coffey met with the prosecutor in his office. After a lengthy demonstration and a review of the evidence, the prosecutor said, "I remember having read something not long ago about the use of fingerprints in law enforcement."

"Our founder, Charles Porter, wrote a ten-page report on the use of fingerprints for *The Law Review* last year," Quill said.

"I remember," the prosecutor said. "I read it."

"Whoever it was who beat that man to death and planted the club in Thornton's hotel room, it wasn't Thornton," Harvey said.

"I'll see the judge and have charges dropped," the prosecutor said.

"Before he's released, we'd like a word with Mr. Thornton," Quill said.

"I can't believe I'm free," Thornton said from his holding cell.

"You can thank these two gentlemen for that," Coffey said.

Thornton looked at Quill and Harvey. "I am in your debt," he said.

"You can do something for us, Mr. Thornton," Quill said.

"If I can," Thornton said.

"Help us find who did kill that man and framed you," Harvey said.

"Who else was in that card game?" Quill said.

An hour later, Quill, Harvey, and Coffey had the five names of the other players and onlookers from the night the man was killed.

"Mr. Thornton, we are releasing you as of this moment, but you must not discuss what happened today with anybody," Quill said. "One word could compromise the chances of finding the real killer. Is this understood?"

"Yes, perfectly," Thornton said.

After Thornton left, Harvey said, "Chief, have your men round up all the names on this list and bring them in for questioning."

By late afternoon, Quill and Harvey had fingerprinted three men from the card game, and not found a match to the billy club.

"We'll print the others in the morning," Quill said.

Coffey's detectives brought in the remaining two players from the game and several spectators from the saloon.

One man's name was Jeff Barr. His thumbprint was a perfect match to the print on the billy club.

Barr was a logger at the same camp as Thornton. The murder had nothing to do with losing at cards. Barr was sweet on a woman Thornton was seeing and, when he saw how drunk Thornton was that night, he took advantage of his condition by murdering the man and planting the club in Thornton's hotel room.

With Thornton out of the way, Barr thought he would have a better chance winning over the woman.

After hearing Barr's confession, the prosecutor charged Barr with murder.

"Boys, can you do me a great favor?" Coffey said. "Can you stay a few extra days and teach my people how to fingerprint?"

"We'll send a wire to the office," Quill said.

CHAPTER FIFTY-SIX

Cavill, Goodluck, and Sato exited the train at the station in Cheyenne, Wyoming.

"Haven't been here in a while," Cavill said.

As they walked through the wide, clean streets of town, Sato said, "It seems like a real nice town."

"It is now," Cavill said. "It was built by the railroad back in sixty-seven. It was a wild and lawless place until a governor was appointed and US Marshals calmed the place down."

"I passed through here several times with the army," Goodluck said. "I barely recognize the place."

"Let's find the marshal," Cavill said.

US Marshall Greg Gates was behind his desk in his office when Cavill, Goodluck, and Sato entered and presented their identification.

"Have a seat, men. I got a fresh pot of

coffee on," Gates said.

After pouring out cups of hot coffee, Gates went back to his desk and rolled a cigarette. "The days of old Cheyenne are long over," he said. "The territorial governor lives here, and there hasn't been a shooting in two years. Most men no longer carry guns, although they haven't been outlawed."

"Tell us what happened," Cavill said.

"The incident took place at the Occidental Saloon a few blocks from here," Gates said. "Two cowboys off a drive got into it over a girl they both saw on the street and took the argument into the saloon. They came to blows and the bouncers tossed them out. The next day, one of them was found dead with a bullet in his liver in the alleyway between the livery and blacksmith shop."

"No one heard the shot?" Cavill said.

"Our doctor said he was killed around three in the morning," Gates said. "In an alley at three a.m., it's possible the shot went unnoticed. I know I didn't hear it."

"A couple of things we need," Cavill said. "The bullet recovered from the body and the gun that you suspect fired it."

"I have the bullet and his gun here in the office," Gates said.

"A question for you, Marshal," Cavill said.

"Why do you have doubts the man is guilty?"

"Not really doubts so much as questions," Gates said. "This man has been on a dozen trail drives to Cheyenne. Like most cowboys on a drive, he lets off steam, gets drunk, has a fight or two, and that's it until next time. I've never really seen any true violence in the man, and I can't believe he'd kill in cold blood over a woman he just met."

"What does the woman say?" Cavill said.

"That she hardly remembers either of them," Gates said.

"We'll do our testing in the morning," Cavill said. "Have you a gunsmith with a target practice range?"

"We do," Gates said.

"We'll be back in the morning," Cavill said.

After checking into the Hotel Cheyenne, Cavill, Goodluck, and Sato ordered baths. Cavill ordered a bottle of whiskey and each man had a drink while they soaked.

Using a hand mirror, Cavill shaved while in the tub. "What do you think of our case, boys?" he said as he scraped stubble.

"Ballistics will prove if the bullet came from his gun," Goodluck said.

"But it doesn't prove that he fired the

gun," Sato said.

"We need to dust the gun for fingerprints, and fingerprint everybody who touched it," Goodluck said.

"Exactly right," Cavill said. "But I'm wondering, just like Gates, why a cowboy off a drive would murder another cowboy in cold blood over a woman he just met."

"That doesn't make much sense, does it?" Goodluck said.

"Affairs of the heart rarely do," Sato said.

"Let's get out of here and get a steak," Cavill said.

CHAPTER FIFTY-SEVEN

Quill and Harvey stood at a table in the meeting room in police headquarters. Coffey introduced them to his two detectives and a dozen of his senior officers.

"Men, I realized that for some of you today is your day off, but the knowledge to be gained here is critical to the performance of your job," Coffey said. "Mr. Quill, Mr. Harvey, the floor is yours."

"Good morning, men," Quill said. "Today you are going to learn the science of finger-printing."

Harvey lifted the suitcase containing the fingerprinting materials to the table.

"Let's start with the basics," Harvey said.

The gunsmith shop had a target range out back. Cavill requested the gunsmith tie a pillow to the target set twenty-one feet from the shooting platform.

"Marshal, hand the gun to Joseph,"

Cavill said.

Gates handed Goodluck the Colt revolver.

"Put six in the pillow," Cavill said.

Goodluck stepped up to the shooting platform. He aimed and fired six rounds into the pillow, making a tight-knit group of bullet holes.

Cavill, Goodluck, Sato, and Gates walked to the target where Cavill dug the six bullets from the target with his penknife.

"Now what?" Gates said.

"We go to your office," Cavill said.

Cavill carefully inspected the six recovered bullets, as did Goodluck and Sato.

"No doubt these six bullets came from his gun," Cavill said. "Marshal, have a look under the microscope. Look at the grooves made by the rifling in the barrel. Compare all six."

After comparing the six bullets, Gates said, "All are a match."

"Let's take a look at the bullet recovered from the body," Cavill said.

Cavill, Goodluck, and Sato all looked at the recovered bullet under the microscope.

"Marshal, have a look," Cavill said.

Gates looked through the microscope at the recovered bullet. "The markings are not even close to matching those other six," he said.

"It doesn't matter how many times you fire his gun. The bullets it shoots will never match the recovered bullet," Cavill said.

"So he didn't do it," Gates said.

"Or he used a different gun," Cavill said.

"The prosecutor said the case was circumstantial at best," Gates said. "Now it isn't even that."

"At least the wrong man won't get hanged," Cavill said.

"Yes, but I have a murder and no suspect," Gates said.

"Can we see the prisoner?" Cavill said.

His name was Willie Loomis. He was in his mid-twenties and had the lean look of career cowboy.

Cavill, Goodluck, Sato, and Gates had Loomis brought to the back room of the jail where he sat at a table.

"Willie, these men are detectives," Gates said. "They want to ask you some questions."

"What kind of questions?" Loomis said.

"About the shooting," Gates said.

"I told you, I didn't shoot anybody," Loomis said.

"Roll up your sleeves," Cavill said.

"What for?" Loomis said.

"It's necessary," Cavill said.

Loomis rolled up his sleeves. Cavill sat opposite him at the table. "Palms up," Cavill said.

Loomis placed his hands on the table, palms up. Cavill put two fingers on the pulse in Loomis's hands.

"What is your name?" Cavill said.

"William Loomis."

"Where are you from?" Cavill said.

"Missouri."

"What do you do for a living?"

"Ranch hand at the Triple T Ranch."

"How long?"

"Three years."

"Did you argue with the victim over a woman?"

"Yes."

"What was it about?"

"We both saw her on the street," Loomis said. "I wanted to ask her to dinner. So did he. We argued. Later, in the bar, we argued some more. He punched me. I punched him back. The bouncers threw us out. That's all I know. I didn't shoot him, and I don't know who did."

"Okay, Willie, thanks," Cavill said.

"What was that all about?" Gates said as he

sat behind his desk.

Cavill sat in a chair and put a cigar between his teeth. "Joseph, you got a Lucifer?"

Goodluck removed a small box of wood matches from his shirt pocket and tossed them to Cavill. The brand name on the matchbox was "Lucifers."

After Cavill lit his cigar, he said, "Marshal Gates, you are aware that all human beings have a pulse."

"Of course," Gates said.

"When you're resting, your pulse beats around seventy-five to eighty times a minute," Cavill said. "When you work hard, exercise, or feel stressed, that number increases. Lying produces stress on the body, which makes the pulse increase. Willie's heart rate never went up a beat."

Gates sighed. "Well, at least we didn't hang an innocent man," he said.

After every man had the opportunity to fingerprint each other, Quill and Harvey took questions and answers for about one hour.

Then they left a supply of fingerprint cards, powders, and brushes with Coffey.

"Buy you men dinner?" Coffey said.

"We have some expense money we need

to burn through," Quill said. "How about we buy you dinner?"

CHAPTER FIFTY-EIGHT

After making coffee in the office, Holt took a walk to the post office for the mail.

As Miss Potts sipped coffee at her desk, she received a telegram from Cavill in Cheyenne. They would be taking the noon train home.

Shortly after that, she received another telegram from Quill and Harvey in Seattle. They were taking the two p.m. train home.

To her surprise, Duffy walked through the door.

Miss Potts jumped to her feet and greeted Duffy with a hug. "Jim, when did you get back?" she said.

"Late last night," Duffy said. "So what's going on around here?"

"Jack, Goodluck, and Mr. Sato are on the way home from Cheyenne, and Quill and Harvey are returning from Seattle," Miss Potts said.

"Good," Duffy said. "We'll need all hands

when we return to Washington. Where is Mr. Holt?"

"Went for the mail," Miss Potts said.

"Any word from Mr. Welding?" Duffy said.

"Yes. He will be here in three weeks," Miss Potts said. "He needed to finish a scouting assignment before his discharge. Jim, you didn't ask, but . . ."

Miss Potts opened a desk drawer and produced the letter from Kathy Bodine.

"Thank you. I'll read it in my office," Duffy said. "Say, is that coffee fresh?"

"Just made."

Duffy went to the pot, filled a cup, and took it to his office. He sat behind his desk, lit a cigar, opened the letter, and read it.

The news wasn't unexpected.

Kathy had decided to stay in Fort Jones. Not because she didn't love him. She did, and she missed him terribly. But she had to stay because she was the only doctor inside of seventy-five square miles, and the people there desperately needed her. In Springfield or Chicago, she would be one of a thousand doctors. In Fort Jones she was the only one.

She ended the letter by telling him she loved him very much and hoped he could find it in his heart to forgive her.

Duffy folded the letter, returned it to the envelope, and stuck it in his desk.

He was about to stand when there was a knock on the door.

"Come," he said.

The door opened and Holt entered the office.

"Glad to see you, Jim," Holt said.

"You're looking well, Lester," Duffy said.

"I expect we have a lot of preparation for Washington," Holt said.

"A great deal," Duffy said. "But I won't go into detail until the others are back."

"Jim, there is no soft way to say this, but I'm going to have to resign my position," Holt said.

"What? Why?" Duffy said.

"The company policy on married men," Holt said.

"You're getting married?" Duffy said.

"That's right," Holt said.

"To whom?" Duffy said.

Miss Potts entered the office. "Me," she said.

Duffy stood up. "That's wonderful," he said.

"What about the policy?" Miss Potts said.

"That was Mr. Porter's policy, not mine," Duffy said. "When is the big day?"

"We figured right after we're finished with the Washington case," Holt said.

"That's fine," Duffy said. "That's just fine."

"Jim, my parents died some time ago," Miss Potts said. "Would you give me away?"

"I'd be honored," Duffy said.

"Well, I think we have some catching up to do if we're going to bring the others up to snuff," Miss Potts said.

CHAPTER FIFTY-NINE

Duffy, Cavill, Goodluck, Sato, Miss Potts, and Holt met in the office meeting room for a briefing.

Miss Potts filled cups with coffee and then took her seat beside Holt.

"On September first, we will have a team on the ship, the captain, US Marshals, and Coast Guard on hand," Duffy said. "Once the money is handed over to the captain, the courier will be arrested. If everything goes to plan, there will be no need for the plan to be repeated on the fifth. Questions?"

"Which of us will be there on the first?" Cavill said.

"Me, Jack, Goodluck, and one other man," Duffy said. "We'll have the second team in Miami in case our plan doesn't work out and the courier doesn't show."

"Valdez?" Goodluck said. "It might be helpful to have him be seen around the pier before dark."

Duffy made a note on a pad. "It's Poule's decision to have him released, but I think he'll see the merit in it. I'll send him a wire today."

"What happens if this courier gives up Maddux?" Cavill said. "Who gets the prize?"

"That will depend on where Maddux is," Duffy said. "If a foreign government is involved, getting him here may take an extradition request, in which case the US Marshals will pick him up at the border."

"That isn't good enough," Cavill said.

"Jack, we already talked about this," Duffy said.

"That son of a bitch is responsible for the murder of Charles Porter and selling who knows how many children into slavery," Cavill said. "We get first crack."

"Jack, listen to me," Duffy said.

"He's right," Goodluck said. "Jack is right."

"He sure is," Holt said.

"I agree," Sato said.

"Jim, we all side with Jack," Miss Potts said.

Duffy sighed as he looked around the table.

"Say no, and we'll all go without you," Cavill said.

"I'll stress the point to Poule, which I have

done already, but I'll do it again," Duffy said.

"Tell him we insist," Cavill said.

"All right. We want to be in Washington around the fifteenth and in Baltimore by the thirtieth," Duffy said. "If nobody objects, that is."

"Nobody objects," Cavill said. "Let's get some lunch."

After lunch at a nearby restaurant, they found Harvey and Quill waiting for them when they returned to the office.

"How did you make out in Seattle?" Duffy said.

Quill and Harvey made a full report about what happened in Seattle.

"Excellent work," Duffy said.

"Where are we with the Washington case?" Quill said.

"Jack, you and the others can take off for the day while I brief Quill and Harvey," Duffy said.

In the backyard of his home, Cavill had fashioned a heavy bag made of leather, filled with one hundred pounds of sand, and hung it from a thick tree branch. In addition, he had barbells, a medicine ball, and jump ropes.

After wrapping his fists in strips of cloth, Cavill pounded away on the heavy bag for the better part of an hour.

Shirtless, dripping sweat, Cavill drank some water and switched over to the barbells.

Sato, dressed in karate gear, joined Cavill in the backyard. While Cavill worked out with the barbells, Sato stretched and did various martial arts routines.

When they paused to drink some water, Cavill said, "Do you think you could teach me to throw those stars?"

"I will get them," Sato said.

A few minutes later, Sato had thrown six stars into the fence in a tight-knit group.

"We need to give you a target," Sato said.

"I've got some whitewash in the basement," Cavill said.

After painting a circle on the fence, Sato instructed Cavill on how to hold and throw a star. After dozens of throws, Cavill was able to put the stars into the center of the target.

"This is a mighty fine weapon," Cavill said.

"It has served my people well for five hundred years," Sato said.

"I'm going to get cleaned up and start thinking about some supper," Cavill said.

"Allow me to cook dinner," Sato said.

"All right," Cavill said.

After a shave, a bath, and a change of clothes, Cavill found Sato in the kitchen,

"Make enough for three. I'm going to get Joseph," Cavill said.

Goodluck's rented apartment in a two-family home was only five blocks away. Cavill covered the distance in a matter of minutes. Goodluck was reading a book when Cavill arrived and gladly accepted the invitation to dinner.

Sato was setting the table in the kitchen when Cavill and Goodluck arrived.

"Please be seated, gentlemen," Sato said. "And I shall serve you dinner."

Sato served tempura, soba, sukiyaki, yakitori, and Japanese wine.

"This is wonderful, Sato," Cavill said. "Really good."

"It puts my native dishes to shame," Goodluck said.

"There's something I want to talk to you about," Cavill said. "I don't trust Poule. He's a politician and if his back's against the wall, he'll cave to save his career."

"I'm not sure I understand what you are saying," Sato said.

"Poule has to please his bosses," Goodluck said. "And he'll do what they tell him to do."

"If he's told to hand over Maddux to a foreign government, he'll do what he's told to do."

"I understand, but if he has to account to his bosses, what can we do about it?" Sato said.

"I for one am not letting someone else punish Maddux for crimes committed against American children, and especially for Porter's murder," Cavill said. "If I have to go it alone, I'll go it alone, but Maddux won't be punished by anyone else but us."

"You won't be alone," Goodluck said.

Cavill looked at Sato.

"No, you won't be," Sato said.

Cavill nodded. "Mr. Porter left Duffy in charge," he said. "Joseph and I are partners, but Jim can terminate us as agents, buy us out, or pay us to do nothing. If that happens, I'm prepared for it. I'll return to fighting full-time and see if I can patch things up with Joey."

"I can return to the army," Goodluck said.

"And I can return to the railroad," Sato said.

"One thing," Goodluck said. "I'm with you all the way except for murder. Even if he deserves it, I won't take part in murder.

We bring him in alive or no deal."

"I'm with Joseph on that one," Sato said.

"Agreed," Cavill said. "Sato, did you make dessert?"

CHAPTER SIXTY

For the next week, Cavill worked out on the heavy bag, lifted weights, and shadowboxed in his yard.

Sato trained Goodluck on martial arts fighting, and Goodluck taught Sato the various ways of Native American fighting.

"How would you fare against Jack?" Goodluck said when he and Sato took a water break.

"Well, first I would try judo," Sato said. "If that didn't work, I would try karate. If that didn't work, I would try jujitsu."

"And if that didn't work?" Goodluck said.

"I'd be left with just two options," Sato said. "The first is to shoot him. The second is to run."

"Shooting him just makes him mad," Goodluck said. "I know. I've seen him get shot, and it doesn't end well for the guy who shot him."

"That leaves the last option," Sato said.

"And the smartest one," Goodluck said.

"Come on, let's practice with the stars," Sato said.

Duffy and Miss Potts spent the week taking care of office paperwork and exchanging telegrams with Poule.

Holt occupied his time working on the mug book.

Quill and Harvey experimented with fingerprint powders, cards, and brushes.

On Monday, except for Miss Potts who stayed behind to monitor the office, the group left for Washington.

There wasn't much to do on the long trip except play cards and read, but Duffy put the time to good use by reviewing every aspect of their plan.

Goodluck read a novel he'd brought along.

Sato wrote several letters to his wife.

Quill, Harvey, and Holt, excellent pool players, spent a great deal of time playing pool in the gentlemen's car.

Cavill spent most of his time playing cards in the gentlemen's car or doing push-ups and sit-ups in his sleeping car.

On Wednesday in the early afternoon, the train arrived in Washington.

They had reservations at a hotel near the

mall. After checking in and getting cleaned up, Duffy sent word to Poule to meet them for dinner at seven o'clock at the hotel.

Duffy reserved a table, and they met Poule at seven in the hotel restaurant.

"Everything seems to be going according to plan," Poule said.

"Cavill, Goodluck, and I will take Baltimore on the first," Duffy said. "Mr. Sato, Holt, Quill, and Harvey will handle Miami," Duffy said.

"A dozen Coast Guard personnel and six US Marshals will be on hand in Baltimore and, if necessary, in Miami," Poule said.

"One thing I'd like to get clear in my mind once and for all," Cavill said. "If we have to work with a foreign government to arrest Maddux, who has jurisdiction?"

"I spoken with the Canadian government on the matter and if need be, we will be allowed into Canada to assist with the arrest," Poule said.

"Assist?" Cavill said.

"Jack," Duffy said.

"Who brings him home?" Cavill said.

"He'll be escorted to the border by the Mounties and turned over to our US Marshals," Poule said.

"Satisfied?" Duffy said.

"Some," Cavill said. "For now."

"I understand how Mr. Cavill feels," Poule said. "Maddux is responsible for hundreds of children being sold into slavery and the murder of your boss. That said, the Justice Department will do everything possible to ensure Maddux is tried and convicted on American soil."

"Now are you satisfied?" Duffy said.

Cavill nodded. "Like I said, for now," he said.

"All right, let's talk about Valdez," Duffy said.

After dinner, Duffy and Cavill sat in chairs on the back porch of the hotel. Each had a glass of whiskey and a cigar.

"Jack, I want to do this right," Duffy said.

"I know," Cavill said.

"We've come a long way the past ten years," Duffy said.

"It doesn't seem that long, does it?" Cavill said.

"No," Duffy said. "I want to tell you this before we leave for Baltimore. I want to do this right because when it's over, I'm going to take some time off."

"Kathy?"

"Yeah. I want to find out if there is anything left between us."

"I was thinking the same about me and

Joey," Cavill said.

"Miss Potts can run things for a while," Duffy said. "And with Holt, Quill and Harvey, Joseph and Sato, they will hardly notice we're gone."

"Don't forget Welding," Cavill said.

"He should be in Springfield by the time this is over," Duffy said. "He'll make a fine addition to the team."

"How long you figure to be gone?"

"A month should do," Duffy said.

"I figure about the same."

"Just do me one favor, please," Duffy said. "Do not kill Maddux on sight."

Cavill sighed.

"Don't pout like a two hundred and fifty pound boy," Duffy said. "Give me your word."

"You have my word," Cavill said.

"Let's find the others and have another drink," Duffy said.

CHAPTER SIXTY-ONE

Baltimore, Maryland, was a major port city and a hub of trade and commerce. It was home to the first railroad, the Baltimore and Ohio, that was built in 1830. It was also home to nearly three hundred and fifty thousand residents.

After checking into a large hotel near the harbor, Duffy, Cavill, and Goodluck took a walk to the harbor.

The privateer ship was in port like a dozen others, seemingly waiting to be loaded with cargo.

After walking the pier, they found a small, outdoor café overlooking the pier that offered a panoramic view of the harbor.

"Poule will be here tonight with Valdez and a team of marshals," Duffy said. "Tomorrow we'll take Valdez for a stroll around the pier and let him be seen by Maddux's invisible people."

"The night of the first, the courier will

most likely make the payment aboard the ship. Who plays the captain?" Cavill said.

"I hate to tell you this, Jack, but Poule said you look like a ship's captain," Duffy said.

"My pleasure," Cavill said.

"Well, we have the rest of the day to ourselves, so if you want to go sightseeing or whatever, we'll meet back at the hotel at seven," Duffy said.

"I'm not much for sightseeing," Cavill said.

"I'd probably scare half the city walking around by myself," Goodluck said.

"How about a game of chess at the hotel?" Duffy said.

"Suits me," Goodluck said.

"I don't want to sound stupid, but what does a ship's captain wear?" Cavill said.

"We can find a store on the way to the hotel," Duffy said.

Cavill tried on the dark pants, white pullover shirt with red, horizontal stripes, and cap in his hotel room.

He stood before the mirror.

"I look like an idiot," he said.

"You look fine," Duffy said.

"You look like a barber pole," Goodluck said.

"Come on, we're meeting Poule in his room," Duffy said.

"Let me change first," Cavill said.

A few minutes later, they met Poule in his room down the hall from theirs.

Valdez and two US Marshals were with Poule in the room.

"We meet again, eh, compadres?" Valdez said.

"Never mind that," Duffy said. "Tomorrow night, the courier arrives with payment. After he pays our man posing as the captain, what usually happens next?"

"He keeps half and gives half to my man waiting on the pier," Valdez said.

"So the courier might look for your man ahead of time?" Duffy said.

"If he's smart," Valdez said.

"We'll have a marshal play the part of Valdez's man just in case," Poule said. "However, the primary target is the courier. He's to be arrested the moment he hands over the money to Mr. Cavill."

"Valdez, have you seen the courier?" Duffy said.

"Yes. Although I never take the money directly from him, I have observed him on several occasions," Valdez said. "From a distance, of course."

"How do you know it's the same man if

you're observing him from a distance?" Poule said.

"Have you not heard of binoculars?" Valdez said.

"I want Valdez in an observation point with us to identify the courier," Duffy said. "And Valdez, don't get any ideas, or that soft one year will turn into a rope. Understand?"

"Perfectly," Valdez said.

"All right. Let's go over the plan one more time," Duffy said.

"I don't see why I need a boatload of marshals to arrest one man," Cavill said as they ate dinner in the hotel restaurant.

"Federal case, federal marshals," Poule said.

"I'd feel better if Joseph was nearby with his bow, just in case we need to take somebody out without alerting half of Baltimore," Duffy said.

Poule looked at Goodluck. "How accurate are you with a bow and from what distance?" he said.

"One hundred yards in the dark, dead center," Goodluck said.

"All right, pick a spot to hide," Poule said. "But stay hidden unless it's necessary for you to shoot."

Goodluck nodded. "We'll take a look first thing tomorrow morning," he said.

"We'll meet for breakfast at seven and review every step," Poule said.

Duffy, Cavill, and Goodluck took glasses of whiskey to the porch of the hotel. The view was that of the harbor. Although it was night, they could see the twinkling of lanterns and candles from ships.

"Is this what white people call the calm before the storm?" Goodluck said.

Cavill lit a cigar and looked at the harbor. "No, Joseph," he said. "Come tomorrow night, we are the storm."

CHAPTER SIXTY-TWO

As Cavill leaned over the deck railing of the privateer ship, he lit a cigar. He had a mug of coffee and quietly sipped from it.

The long harbor was dark, with a sprinkling of lanterns on various ships. Although sailors weren't visible, sound traveled far at night, and he could hear muffled conversations.

He couldn't see them, but hidden among the buildings and ships were a dozen Coast Guard personnel, Duffy, Goodluck, Poule, and Valdez.

Below deck, six US Marshals waited in hiding.

Cavill puffed on the cigar and sipped coffee. His eyes scanned the darkness, his ears listened for the sound of footsteps.

The time was just past midnight.

He waited, watching and listening. Fog rolled in, casting the pier in a cloudlike mist.

Cup empty, Cavill went below to refill it

and then went topside to continue his watch.

Cigar spent, he tossed it overboard.

About to light another, Cavill paused when he heard faint footsteps on the dock. He watched the fog. A lone figure emerged. He was tall and slender, dressed in black.

The lone figure walked to the privateer ship, stopped, and looked at Cavill.

"A nice night for a walk," the lone figure said.

"Indeed," Cavill said. "May I offer you some coffee?"

"You may," the lone figure said.

The lone figure crossed the gangplank to the ship's deck.

"Below in the galley," Cavill said. "After you."

They went below and turned right to the galley. A pot of coffee rested on the large woodstove.

"Are you Maddux's man?" Cavill said.

"Indeed I am," the courier said.

Cavill filled a mug with coffee and handed it to the courier.

"Thank you, sir," the courier said. He took a sip, set the cup on the table, and then lifted his shirt to remove a money belt. "Best count it before I leave," he said.

Cavill opened the money belt and looked

at the thick stack of money. "Who said you're leaving?" he said.

Six marshals with guns drawn rushed into the galley.

The courier looked at Cavill. "You, sir, are no gentleman," he said.

The captured courier sat and stared at the wall for the better part of thirty minutes while Poule and Duffy asked him questions.

When he finally spoke, he said, "May I roll a cigarette?"

"You're not grasping the situation very well, are you?" Poule said. "We have Valdez and two of your ships and their captains. We have you red-handed with the payoff money. We know the man at the head of the table is William Maddux."

"So why are you bothering with me?" the courier said.

"Because what we don't have is the location where Maddux hangs his hat," Duffy said.

The courier laughed. "And I should tell you why?" he said.

"Because if you don't, your best outcome is to die in prison somewhere around 1930," Duffy said. "And your worst outcome is to hang by the neck until dead. Neither is very appealing, if you were to ask me."

"You're trying to scare me," the courier said. "It won't work."

"No? Too bad," Duffy said. "Because it might take some time to trace the money we recovered from your belt using the serial numbers to its origin, but eventually we will, and you will spend life in prison or be hanged, when neither of those outcomes was necessary. Come on, Tom, let him rot."

Duffy and Poule stood up and walked to the locked door. "Guard," Duffy said.

"Wait," the courier said.

Duffy and Poule turned around. "Yes?" Poule said.

"How much time will I do if I talk?" the courier said.

"We'll give you the same deal we gave Valdez," Poule said. "One year."

"I could do a year," the courier said.

Poule and Duffy took their seats. Poule removed a pad and pencil from his briefcase. "Start talking. Begin with your name," Poule said.

"William Maddux, Junior," the courier said.

Duffy and Poule stared at Maddux Jr.

"I figure Dad is old and I'm not," Maddux Jr. said. "Why should he die of old age a rich man while I get my neck stretched."

"Jesus Christ," Poule said.

"So where is dear old dad living these days?" Duffy said.

"His primary residence is just north of Montreal in the country," Maddux Jr. said. "Being from the south, he hates the cold. He has a winter home where he is right now."

"And where is that?" Poule said.

Maddux Jr. smiled. "My Daddy didn't raise a fool. That's all you get without I see something in writing."

Poule reached into his briefcase for the typed document agreeing to a one year deal in exchange for Maddux. "Read it," he said.

Maddux Jr. read every word and then said, "Have you pen and ink?"

Poule removed an ink bottle from his briefcase and a tipped pen. After Maddux signed the document, Poule did the same.

"Now tell us where we can find your father," Poule said.

"Cuba," Maddux Jr. said.

Duffy, Cavill, Goodluck, and Poule went to breakfast at a restaurant near the harbor.

"After we get some sleep, we'll return to Washington and find the exact location of Maddux's winter home on a map," Poule said. "And I will wire our embassy in Havana."

"Will they allow us to go in and arrest him ourselves?" Duffy said.

"Probably not," Poule said. "Cuba is an unstable government at the moment. Civil War could erupt at any moment. We might have to rely upon the federal police to make the arrest."

"Are you that naïve to think Maddux hasn't bribed them to allow him to stay there?" Cavill said.

"No, I'm not," Poule said. "But I'm not willing to risk a war with Spain over Bill Maddux. After we get to Washington, I'll speak with the president. Right now I think we all need some sleep."

CHAPTER SIXTY-THREE

"I knew he'd waver when it came to the end," Cavill said as he ate some eggs.

"He didn't, Jack," Duffy said. "He said he's not willing to start a war with Spain by invading Cuba."

"Who said anything about invading?" Cavill said. "I'm talking about one man, a war criminal and a slaver, being brought to justice."

"Jack, in all likelihood Maddux has bribed Cuban officials to allow him to live there in the winter," Duffy said. "He traded slaves there until 1870, so he must know every corrupt official on the entire island."

"He can't be alone," Goodluck said. "He must have people with him. Protection. Soldiers, maybe. Maybe private guns for hire."

"I'm sure he's well protected," Duffy said.

"What time are we meeting Poule?" Cavill said.

"Five o'clock," Duffy said.

"Then after breakfast, I'm going to get some sleep," Cavill said.

Poule had a large map of Cuba spread out on the conference table in his office. Standing at the table with Poule were Duffy, Cavill, Goodluck, and Maddux Jr.

"Show me on the map where your father's home is located," Poule said.

Maddux Jr. put his finger on the map. "Here," he said. "In Santiago de Cuba, on the hillside. It is quite beautiful. The city is very large, but the countryside is sparse, made up of plantations. The city itself is considered a major seaport."

"Is that why your father chose it, for the port?" Poule said.

"Partly. Slavery wasn't abolished until five years after the Civil War," Maddux Jr. said. "He was already well established in Cuba by then, so he moved operations there in sixty-one, I believe. He was young then, like I am now."

"When did he go to Montreal?" Poule said.

"In sixty-three," Maddux Jr. said. "Our family's roots go back to Canada, and he is fluent in French as well as Spanish. He thought America would never look for him in Montreal, and he was right. You never did."

"Where is his house on the map?" Duffy said.

"Here," Maddux Jr. said, pointing. "Between these hills."

"What's the layout of the house, and how many men does he have with him?" Duffy said.

"The house is large with a deck that faces the sun," Maddux Jr. said. "There is a guesthouse in the rear for the men that aren't on duty. Usually there are eight to twelve men, all armed. There is also a cook and a housekeeper."

"Can you see the road from the house?" Duffy said.

"The road curves, so you can see the part that leads to the house," Maddux Jr. said. "The rest is hidden by the hills."

"You are going to draw a map of the road, the hills, everything," Duffy said.

Maddux nodded.

"And keep in mind that if you double-cross us, it means a rope or life," Duffy said.

"When did I give you the impression I was stupid?" Maddux Jr. said.

Duffy set a pad and pencil on the table. "Map," he said.

Maddux Jr. started to sketch on the pad.

"Here is the road through the hills," he said. "On the left are some coffee and tobacco plantations. Here is the turn where you can first see the house."

"How far to the house?" Duffy said.

"Maybe a quarter-mile along the road," Maddux Jr. said.

"Are the hills passable?" Duffy said.

"If you are stout enough," Maddux Jr. said.

"You said there were coffee and tobacco plantations," Duffy said.

"Coffee only grows on the hills and mountains," Maddux Jr. said.

"I know that," Duffy said. "Are there people working the fields?"

"During picking time," Maddux Jr. said. "It is not picking time."

"How far from the port to the house?" Duffy said.

"Maybe four miles."

"Where were the ships headed had we not intercepted them?" Duffy said.

"The ship in Baltimore was headed for Jamaica," Maddux Jr. said. "The other for the Orient somewhere."

"How do you let your father know the ships sailed?" Duffy said.

"Telegram."

"What do you write?" Duffy said.

"The cargo has left port."

"That's it?"

"That's it."

"To where?"

"William Maddux, Santiago de Cuba," Maddux Jr. said.

Duffy looked at Poule, and Poule nodded.

"Are you hungry?" Duffy said.

"Yes, very," Maddux said.

"Let's break for dinner," Duffy said.

After sending a telegram to Maddux in Santiago de Cuba, Poule joined Duffy, Cavill, and Goodluck at the table.

"When he gets the telegram, he'll have no reason to doubt it because it came from Baltimore," Poule said.

"Have you heard back from the president?" Duffy said.

"Not yet," Poule said. "But after we're done with Jr. there, we'll head back to Washington and see him first thing."

"He better not screw it up," Cavill said.

"Jack, Arthur can only go so far without starting a war with Spain," Duffy said.

"Do you really think Spain is so stupid as to start a war with America over some slave trader?" Cavill said.

"You have to understand diplomatic relations," Poule said.

"No, *you* have to understand that if you fail to get cooperation from the Cuban government, *I* will go alone as a private citizen," Cavill said. "Cuba is an open country. If I want a little vacation and to buy my cigars firsthand, there is nothing you can do to stop me."

Poule looked at Duffy.

"I can stop you," Poule said. "I can have you arrested for violating an executive order and invading a sovereign country. That's treason. Do you know the penalty for treason, Mr. Cavill?"

Cavill stood up from the table and glared at Poule. "You stinking rat," he said.

"Before you go nuts, Jack, listen to what Tom has to say," Duffy said.

Slowly, Cavill took his seat.

"We want Maddux and the others to pay for Charles Porter's murder as much as you do," Poule said. "But when he is captured, we need the goodwill of who knows how many foreign governments to ensure the return of who knows how many kidnapped children Maddux sold into slavery. Now if you can't understand that, I will have you arrested this very evening and imprisoned."

"He's very good at making a point," Goodluck said.

"Jack?" Duffy said.

"Yeah, okay," Cavill said.

"Let's get back to Junior," Poule said.

"How was your dinner?" Poule said.

"Excellent," Maddux Jr. said.

"We have just a few more questions," Duffy said.

"Sure," Maddux Jr. said as he rolled a cigarette.

"How old are you?" Duffy said.

"Twenty-three," Maddux Jr. said.

"Born after your father fled the country?" Duffy said.

"I was told I was born in Cuba, but I have no proof of that," Maddux Jr. said. "My mother died in Montreal when I was very young."

"When did you start working with your father in the slave-trading business?" Duffy said.

"Soon after my eighteenth birthday."

"Five years. You must know the business pretty well," Duffy said.

"All I do for my father is deliver money to the ships' captains," Maddux Jr. said.

"So you must have a pretty good idea of the ships' destinations," Duffy said.

Poule looked at Duffy and nodded.

"Some," Maddux Jr. said.

"Make a list of all countries involved that

you can remember," Duffy said.

"In exchange for?"

"Two months off the one year," Poule said.

"Give me a pad and pencil," Maddux said.

Duffy, Cavill, Goodluck, and Poule sat in chairs on the porch of the hotel with glasses of whiskey.

Cavill lit a cigar and said, "Be nice to see where my cigars come from."

"The eight o'clock train gets us into D.C. by ten," Poule said. "I'll see the president at noon. Stand by in case he wishes to see you."

"We'll be standing by," Duffy said.

"Let's hope that's not all we're doing," Cavill said.

Chapter Sixty-Four

"I can't stand this waiting," Cavill said.

"It's only been an hour," Duffy said.

"Who wants more coffee?" Goodluck said.

"Bring us a pot," Duffy said.

Goodluck stood up from his chair on the hotel porch and entered the hotel.

Cavill emptied his coffee cup and lit a cigar. "God, I hate this city," he said.

"I'm not too fond of it myself," Duffy said.

"Has he made you a firm offer yet?" Cavill said.

Duffy looked at Cavill.

"I'm not stupid, Jim. Neither is Joseph."

"Remember we talked about taking a month off to see our girls?" Duffy said.

"I remember."

"That's the only plan I have," Duffy said.

Goodluck returned with a coffeepot and filled the cups. "Miss Potts sent a telegram to the hotel," he said and handed the wire to Duffy.

"I wired her when we checked in," Duffy said.

"I never thought I'd be glad to see Springfield," Cavill said. "Washington is a rat swamp."

A horse-drawn coach arrived curbside. The driver stepped down and walked to the porch. "Would one of you gents be James Duffy?" he said.

"That's me," Duffy said.

"I'm instructed to take you and your associates to the White House," the driver said.

President Chester Arthur sat behind his desk in the Oval Office, while Poule, Duffy, Cavill, and Goodluck sat opposite him in chairs.

"The Justice Department has been searching for William Maddux since sixty-five," Arthur said. "I've been in constant contact with our embassy in Havana by telegram since yesterday. The Cuban government is not going to take action to arrest Maddux."

"How can they . . . ?" Cavill said.

Arthur held up his right hand to quiet him. "They will, however, look the other way if we wish to go in and remove him ourselves."

Poule looked at Duffy, Cavill, and Goodluck. "How do you men feel about that?" he said.

"This is a job for a select few," Duffy said.

"Do you men know any select few?" Arthur said.

"Me," Cavill said.

"And me," Goodluck said.

"Damn right," Duffy said.

"A cargo ship manned by Coast Guard personnel will take you to the port of Santiago de Cuba," Poule said. "They will not set foot on land, because placing our military on their soil can be taken as an act of war."

"When is the next full moon?" Duffy said.

"The next . . . I don't know," Poule said.

"Get me an aide," Arthur said.

Poule went to the door, opened it and motioned, and an aide rushed in. "Yes sir," he said.

"When is the next full moon?" Arthur said.

"The next . . . I don't know, sir," the aide said.

"Wire the *Post* and ask them," Arthur said. "They keep track of those sorts of things. Tell them it's for me."

"Right away," the aide said and dashed out of the office.

"Now suppose you tell me why you need

to know the phases of the moon," Arthur said.

Duffy opened his briefcase and removed a map of Cuba and the hand-drawn map Maddux Jr. made. He placed them on the desk.

"The road to the Maddux home in the hills is visible from the road from a quarter-mile off," Duffy said. "We have to travel at night without lanterns. A full moon will make it a lot easier."

"I see," Arthur said. "Tom, have you offered these men positions at Justice?"

"Working on it, sir," Poule said.

"Justice always needs good men," Arthur said.

There was a knock on the door and Poule opened it to let the aide in. "In eighteen days the moon will be full," he said.

"Thank you," Arthur said. "Tom, get someone from the Coast Guard."

The Admiral of the Coast Guard sat beside Duffy in the Oval Office and listened to the plan Duffy outlined.

"The ship will be a cargo ship, but the only cargo on board will be us three," Duffy said. "The entire crew will be Coast Guard personnel. Once we land in Santiago de Cuba, you won't be allowed on land, but you will be allowed to wait for us to return."

"And the objective is?" the admiral said.

"Classified until you reach Cuba," Arthur said.

"The moon is full in eighteen days and will last for three days," Duffy said. "How long will it take to reach Santiago?"

"From Baltimore, traveling at twelve to fifteen knots, about ninety six hours," the admiral said.

"We'll leave in thirteen days," Duffy said.

"Mr. President, I expect my men to carry full arms," the admiral said.

"Just so long as those guns are not seen in Cuba," Arthur said.

"Once we are back on board, we will leave immediately for Baltimore," Duffy said.

The admiral nodded. "I'll make all arrangements with my staff," he said.

"We will meet here when you have made arrangements to finalize the plan," Arthur said.

"Yes sir," the admiral said.

"Mr. Duffy, are you and your men free for dinner?" Arthur said.

CHAPTER SIXTY-FIVE

The White House chef prepared baked chicken with roasted potatoes, carrots, and corn with a first course of French onion soup.

White wine was served with the meal.

"You men realize this is going to be a violent mission," Arthur said.

"Yes sir," Duffy said.

"We figure we're going to have to fight our way in and possibly out," Cavill said.

"And the thought of possibly getting killed doesn't frighten you?" Arthur said.

"Jim and I have been in a hundred gunfights during the past ten years, and Joseph has been in wars since he was ten," Cavill said. "If shooting guns frightened us, we'd retire."

"Mr. Goodluck, I find you most interesting," Arthur said. "First you fought against the white man and then joined his army. You speak your native language, English,

French, and Spanish, read extensively, and play chess. I find you most amazing."

"He shoots a mean game of pool, too," Cavill said.

"And you, Mr. Cavill. I'm told you are a superior boxer," Arthur said.

"I saw him spar with Sullivan in San Francisco recently," Goodluck said. "My money would be on Jack."

"And Mr. Duffy, you aspire to be a lawyer," Arthur said.

"Someday," Duffy said.

"You are very interesting and qualified men," Arthur said. "I hope you will all consider Tom's offer seriously."

"I told Tom we won't discuss it until after the mission is complete," Duffy said.

"My hope is that you men want to see justice done and not revenge," Arthur said. "Justice is a very difficult thing to achieve. Revenge is easy."

"Mr. President, our goal is to bring Maddux back alive to stand trial for murder, slave trading, kidnapping, and child sex trafficking," Duffy said. "I want him to rot in prison or be hanged by a jury of his peers."

"Mr. Cavill, Mr. Goodluck, I'm sure you feel the same," Arthur said.

"Mr. President, the bad guys don't always give you a choice," Cavill said.

"No, indeed," Arthur said. "Well, my chef has made us a chocolate layer cake that I am most anxious to try."

"So what do we do for thirteen days?" Cavill said. "If I stay around here, I'll go crazy."

"You and Joseph could take a trip home for a few days," Duffy said.

"Another week on a train? No thanks," Cavill said.

"Joseph?" Duffy said.

"Let's go hunting for a few days," Goodluck said. "I understand that Maryland has some good hunting grounds."

"Not a bad idea, Joseph," Cavill said. "Jim?"

"I could use a few days of fresh air," Duffy said. "I'll tell Tom in the morning."

"That reminds me," Cavill said. "All that talk about Poule offering us jobs. He offered you a job, not us."

"Politics, Jack," Duffy said. "This is Washington."

"Mr. Porter never cared for politics, Jim," Cavill said. "And neither do I."

"I can't say as I'm all that fond of politics myself," Duffy said.

"We should find out where we can go hunting tomorrow and just go," Goodluck said.

"I agree," Duffy said. "We'll need gear and food for a few days, but I'm sure we can find that right here."

"Let's get a drink," Cavill said. "I'm tired of sitting on this stupid hotel porch."

At the hotel bar, Duffy ordered three glasses of whiskey.

"I heard western Maryland has some good hunting grounds," Goodluck said. "A lot of whitetail in those woods."

A man at the bar walked closer to Goodluck. "Excuse me, gentlemen, but did I hear you say you were going hunting?" he said.

"We'd like to," Goodluck said.

"I'm guessing you're from out of town," the man said.

"We're visiting," Duffy said.

"Maryland is a permit state," the man said. "You'll need to apply for an out-of-state permit to hunt."

"A permit? To hunt a deer?" Cavill said.

"It could take weeks," the man said.

"Thanks for the information," Duffy said.

"Sure," the man said.

"Joseph, let's go home for a few days," Cavill said.

CHAPTER SIXTY-SIX

Miss Potts greeted Cavill and Goodluck with a warm hug. Holt shook their hands.

"I couldn't stand all that sitting around, so we figured we'd come home for a few days," Cavill said.

"Where are the others?" Goodluck said.

"Quill, Harvey, and Mr. Sato are in Sacramento looking at offices," Miss Potts said. "Why didn't Jim come with you?"

"He's playing politics," Cavill said.

"Don't be too hard on him, Jack," Miss Potts said. "We need friends in Washington if we are to get our fingerprint and ballistics experiments accepted as normal practices."

"Give me a good old-fashioned cattle theft anytime," Cavill said. "Joseph, let's get going."

"Where?" Miss Potts said.

"Hunting," Cavill said.

Cavill and Goodluck rode their horses deep

into the woods and dismounted. Each brought his Colt sidearm, Winchester rifle, and the throwing stars Sato had given them.

"We need a target," Cavill said.

"That wide oak over there," Goodluck said.

Cavill counted out twenty-five feet from the wide oak tree. Then he turned, drew his Colt, and fired six shots into the tree in a tight-knit group.

As he reloaded, Goodluck drew his Colt and fired six shots in a group nearly as tight as Cavill's.

"Good shooting, Joseph," Cavill said.

"Let's try the stars," Goodluck said.

For several hours they practiced with the throwing stars until each man could make a tight circle with them in the oak tree.

They stopped to build a fire, make a pot of coffee, and cook the steaks they'd brought from town. As the steaks cooked, Goodluck opened a can of beans and stirred them into a separate pan. Cavill added an ounce of bourbon for flavor.

"Joseph, the west is dying," Cavill said. "Pretty soon it will be filled with homes with picket fences and gardens and fenced-in ranges, and outlaws will be a thing of the past."

"My people started saying that two hundred years ago," Goodluck said. "And it may be true, but outlaws will always be with us. Of that I am certain."

"Maybe so, but I don't plan on chasing them the rest of my life," Cavill said.

"Let's eat. You'll feel better."

After lunch, they practiced with their Winchester rifles from a distance of fifty feet from the oak tree.

Both men were excellent shots.

"Not that you need it, but why don't you practice a bit with your bow?" Cavill said.

"What do you think Jim is doing right now?" Goodluck said.

"Jim, this is Coast Guard Captain Ed O'Neal," Poule said. "Ed, Jim Duffy."

Duffy and O'Neal shook hands.

"I'll be piloting your ship to Cuba," O'Neal said. "My crew of twelve will all be officers. In addition to supplies for the trip, we will be carrying a full battery of weapons. Below deck, of course."

"Captain, I'd like to suggest dinner with you and your crew tomorrow night so that they can meet Jim," Poule said. "After all, none of this would be possible without him."

"Name the time and place," O'Neal said.

After O'Neal left Poule's office, Duffy said, "Tom, I'd like to talk to you about our fingerprint and ballistics program."

"Plenty of time for that after you return from Cuba," Poule said.

"But I have the entire week free," Duffy said. "You could get me before the Senate tomorrow if you wanted to."

"Yes, but I don't want you focused on anything but Maddux right now," Poule said. "When you return from Cuba, I'll make arrangements."

"All right, Tom," Duffy said.

"Good. Let's get some lunch," Poule said.

CHAPTER SIXTY-SEVEN

Poule and Duffy arrived at some senator's home at seven o'clock. By seven-thirty, Duffy was ready to leave.

"Tom, this is the fourth party this week," Duffy said.

"This is when deals get made, Jim," Poule said. "Nothing happens in Washington until the sun goes down."

"I'm not interested in . . ." Duffy said.

"Do you see those two men over there in the corner?" Poule said. "They are drunk. They have their arms around each other and are singing."

"I see them," Duffy said.

"One is a Democrat. The other is a Republican," Poule said. "During the day they fight like mortal enemies, calling each other names and even coming to blows. But at night, they get drunk together, sing a few songs, and in the morning they will work together on some bill or another."

"Tom, I leave for Cuba in three days," Duffy said. "I need to be sharp and alert. I can't risk the lives of the other men by being in a whiskey-soaked haze. I'm going back to the hotel."

"The host will be insulted," Poule said.

"The host isn't going to Cuba," Duffy said. "I'll be leaving for Baltimore tomorrow morning."

When Duffy stepped out of the taxi, he was delighted to see Cavill and Goodluck on the porch with mugs of coffee.

"Where did you get the dude suit?" Cavill said.

"It's what all fashionable men wear after dark in D.C., don't you know that?" Duffy said.

Duffy walked up to the porch and sat in a chair beside Goodluck.

"Want some coffee?" Goodluck said.

"I would love some," Duffy said.

Goodluck entered the hotel.

"If you don't mind me saying, Jim, Washington life doesn't seem to suit you," Cavill said.

"Don't I know it," Duffy said.

Goodluck returned with a mug of coffee and gave it to Duffy.

"Thank you, Joseph," Duffy said.

351

"When do we get out of here?" Cavill said.

"Tomorrow morning we take the train for Baltimore," Duffy said.

"Thank God for that," Cavill said.

"How are things at home," Duffy said.

"Quill, Harvey, and Sato are in Sacramento looking for offices," Cavill said.

"Good," Duffy said.

A cab arrived curbside. Poule got out and came up to the porch. "Jim, the Coast Guard ship is already in the harbor in Baltimore," he said.

"We'll meet it there tomorrow," Duffy said.

"A moment in private," Poule said.

"Come on, Joseph, let's play a game of pool before we turn in," Cavill said.

Cavill and Goodluck entered the hotel. Poule took Goodluck's chair.

"People are upset with you, Jim," Poule said. "Senators and congressmen wanted to talk to you tonight. Your early departure took some smoothing over."

"We leave for Cuba in three days, Tom," Duffy said. "Maybe one of us, or all three of us, will be killed trying to apprehend Maddux. At the moment, I really don't give a damn about how upset they are."

"Understandable," Poule said. "I'll travel with you to Baltimore in the morning.

Goodnight, Jim."

"Goodnight, Tom," Duffy said.

Duffy entered the hotel and found Cavill and Goodluck shooting pool in the gaming room.

Cavill banked a shot and looked at Duffy. "Don't trust that man, Jim," he said. "He's looking for a reputation any way he can get one."

"He's riding with us to Baltimore," Duffy said.

"Maybe he'll ride with us to Cuba, and I can throw him overboard," Cavill said.

"Wishful thinking," Goodluck said.

CHAPTER SIXTY-EIGHT

"That's your ship," Poule said as he, Duffy, Cavill, and Goodluck walked from the taxi to the harbor.

"It looks big enough for thirty men," Cavill said.

"It is," Poule said.

They reached the ship. O'Neal was out front to greet them.

"Ed, you remember Jim Duffy?" Poule said.

"Of course," O'Neal said as he shook Duffy's hand.

"The big fellow is Jack Cavill," Poule said. "And this is Joseph Goodluck."

O'Neal shook their hands. "Welcome aboard, men," he said.

"Godspeed," Poule said. "And safe return."

"Come on board," O'Neal said. "And we'll get underway."

The sleeping quarters below deck held twenty hammocks. The detectives stored their gear and met O'Neal on deck.

"Sorry about the sleeping quarters, men," O'Neal said. "It's all a ship like this has, except for officers' lodging."

"Don't trouble yourself, Captain," Duffy said.

"When do we get underway?" Cavill said.

"Now," O'Neal said.

"I've never been on a ship," Goodluck said.

"Don't worry about it," O'Neal said. "The ship does the work. All we do is point her in the right direction."

"Is there coffee somewhere?" Cavill said.

"Galley below deck," O'Neal said. "The cook will make some as soon as we're underway."

Duffy, Cavill, and Goodluck stood by the railing and watched as the ship pulled away from the dock and entered Baltimore Harbor.

Thirty minutes later, O'Neal joined them on deck. "It's a fine day to set sail," he said. "Hardly any swells at all."

"What are swells?" Goodluck said.

"That slight up and down motion of the ship as it passes over the water," O'Neal said. "If you look over the edge you can see it."

Goodluck peered over the railing. "I don't feel too well," he said.

"That's right. It's your first time at sea," O'Neal said. "There's a bucket in the stern."

"What's a stern?" Goodluck said.

"The rear," O'Neal said.

"If you need me, I'll be with the bucket," Goodluck said.

Duffy and Cavill were having lunch at the captain's table with O'Neal when a haggard-looking Goodluck came in and sat down.

"Mr. Goodluck, have some of these," O'Neal said as he set a bowl of peppermint candy on the table.

"Candy?" Goodluck said.

"Peppermint. A seaman's best friend," O'Neal said. "Settles the stomach."

Goodluck reached for a peppermint stick and bit off a piece.

While Duffy and Cavill slept in hammocks, Goodluck reached below to the bowl of peppermint candies on the floor and picked one up. He bit off a piece and looked up at the ceiling.

A lantern on the wall illuminated the sleeping quarters enough for him to see, and Goodluck looked at Duffy and Cavill. Both men were sound asleep.

Goodluck stood up from the cot, grabbed several sticks of peppermint, left the sleeping quarters, and went topside.

The night air was cooler, crisp with the smell of salt in it. The ship's deck was lit by lanterns, but the sea was pitch-black except for the shimmering patch where moonlight lit it up like a watery blanket.

Goodluck looked overhead at the millions of stars.

"It's quite an experience, your first night at sea," O'Neal said.

"I was just thinking that," Goodluck said.

"How is your stomach?" O'Neal said.

"The peppermint helps."

"Good," O'Neal said. "By the time we reach Santiago, you'll have your sea legs."

"Sea legs?"

"When you wake up hungry instead of sick, you'll have your sea legs," O'Neal said.

CHAPTER SIXTY-NINE

"I didn't think anybody but you could eat that much, Jack," Duffy said.

As he ate a spoonful of scrambled eggs, Goodluck said, "Captain O'Neal said I have my sea legs."

"I'm going topside," Cavill said.

"I'll join you," Duffy said. "Joseph?"

"I'll be along," Goodluck said.

On deck, Duffy and Cavill found O'Neal portside.

"When do we reach Santiago, Captain?" Duffy said.

"We should be there by eight tonight," O'Neal said.

"According to your charts, the moon is at full zenith at ten o'clock," Duffy said.

"That gives us plenty of time to walk the four miles of road to Maddux's house," Cavill said.

"I wish my men and I could accompany you, but orders are orders," O'Neal said.

"We wouldn't dream of asking you to violate them, Captain," Duffy said.

"I'm going to check my gear and take a nap," Cavill said.

"Good idea," Duffy said.

"I have dinner set for six o'clock," O'Neal said.

"See you then," Duffy said.

Cavill stripped, cleaned and loaded his Colt Peacemaker, then checked his Winchester rifle.

"Jack, you've cleaned your weapons twice already since we've been on this ship," Duffy said.

"I will not die due to mechanical failure," Cavill said.

Duffy and Goodluck got into their cots.

"Best get some sleep, Jack," Duffy said. "We have a long night ahead of us."

"Your cook knows his way around a steak," Cavill said.

"Like the army, the Coast Guard travels on its stomach," O'Neal said.

"How far to Santiago?" Goodluck said.

"We've been in Cuban waters since this morning," O'Neal said. "We'll dock at eight tonight. Sunset is in one hour, if you're interested in viewing this spectacle over Cuba."

Although Cuba was at least three miles away, the sheer size of the island dominated the horizon.

Duffy, Cavill, Goodluck, and O'Neal watched as the setting sun cast the island in a pinkish glow.

"Someday, when I have retired from service, what I will miss the most are the sunrises and sunsets," O'Neal said.

"I can understand why," Duffy said.

"We dock in forty-five minutes," O'Neal said.

The Cuban authorities from Havana came aboard to speak with O'Neal before allowing Duffy, Cavill, and Goodluck to set foot on land.

"When you return, if you return, we won't be here," one of the Cuban officials said in English.

"Well," Duffy said. "Let's get to it."

Each holding a Winchester rifle and a canteen of water, Duffy, Cavill, and Goodluck walked across the gangplank to Cuba.

Slung across Goodluck's back was his bow and a fully loaded quiver.

Chapter Seventy

Except for Duffy, Cavill, and Goodluck, the road was deserted. The full moon overhead made it fairly easy to traverse, and they made good time walking at a steady pace.

Cavill lit a cigar. "This might be the stupidest thing we've ever done," he said. "I feel like Daniel walking into the lion's den."

"I didn't know you read scripture," Duffy said.

"Every Sunday at the orphanage," Cavill said.

"As I recall, Daniel was saved by God because God found Daniel to be blameless," Goodluck said.

"I wouldn't exactly call Jack blameless," Duffy said.

Cavill paused.

"What?" Duffy said.

"That looks like tobacco growing there," Cavill said.

"I believe it is," Duffy said.

Cavill looked at his cigar and said, "That's your relatives over there."

Goodluck reached into his pocket for a peppermint stick.

"Jesus, Joseph, we're on land," Cavill said.

"I sort of developed a taste for peppermint," Goodluck said.

"Let me have one," Duffy said.

Goodluck gave Duffy a peppermint stick.

"Jack?" Goodluck said.

"I'll try one," Cavill said.

They munched peppermint sticks as they walked, silent for a few minutes. The night air was hot, almost sweltering, and the three of them sweated through their shirts.

"I got to say Cuba is one hot place at night," Cavill said. "How does anybody get any work done around here?"

"They're born into it," Duffy said. "Like the Eskimo people in Alaska."

"I read a book on Alaska," Goodluck said. "They say it will become an official territory soon."

"Too cold for me," Cavill said. "I heard they get minus fifty degrees there in the winter."

"I would like to see the icebergs and the cliffs of ice a mile thick," Goodluck said.

"Let me get another of those peppermint sticks," Cavill said.

"Jim?" Goodluck said.

"I'll take another one," Duffy said.

Two peppermint sticks later, they reached the curve in the road where the Maddux home became visible. A faint outline in moonlight, the porch was well lit by hanging lanterns.

To their right was the hill Maddux Jr. described on the map.

"Shall we?" Duffy said.

The hill was long, with a low-level grade that topped out at around one thousand feet.

When they reached the top of the hill, they looked down upon the house from about three hundred feet away.

Two men were on the porch as night watchmen. Twelve horses were in the corral to the left of the house.

"Joseph, how close do you need to be for a night shot on those two?" Duffy whispered.

"A hundred and fifty feet," Goodluck whispered.

"Spread out and keep in the shadows," Duffy said.

They moved fifteen feet apart and walked slowly down the hill until they were about one hundred and fifty feet away from the large house.

Duffy looked at Goodluck and nodded.

Goodluck removed four arrows from his quiver and put two arrows in the chests of both men.

Duffy and Cavill ran to Goodluck.

"Now," Duffy said.

Cavill removed the flask of whiskey from his boot. Duffy pulled the strips of cloth from his gear bag and wrapped them around four of Goodluck's arrows. Cavill soaked the strips with whiskey, struck a match, and ignited them one at a time as Goodluck fired them onto the roof of the house.

It didn't take long for the roof to catch fire and spread.

"Give them a few more," Duffy said. "The walls, if you can hit them."

Goodluck put two flaming arrows into the walls on each side of the front door. Within seconds the roof and walls were engulfed in tall flames.

The horses in the corral bucked and panicked.

"Do not shoot Maddux," Duffy said.

The front door opened and men ran out to the porch and jumped to the ground, coughing and hacking.

"At their feet," Duffy said.

Duffy, Cavill, and Goodluck fired their Winchesters at the feet of the men in front of the house.

"Goodluck, tell them that any man who moves will be shot," Duffy said.

Joseph cupped his hands and shouted in Spanish.

One man ran to the corral. Cavill shot him with his Winchester.

"Joseph, tell them all we want is Maddux, that we do not want to kill anyone else," Duffy said.

Goodluck cupped his hands again and shouted in Spanish.

One man shouted back in Spanish.

Goodluck said, "He said they will do as you say."

"Tell them to get in the corral and to wait," Duffy said.

Goodluck shouted in Spanish.

The men walked to the corral and got in with the horses.

"The fire lights things up considerably, doesn't it?" Cavill said.

"Let's go," Duffy said.

They walked down the hill with rifles at the ready until they reached the corral.

"English?" Duffy said.

"Yes," one man said.

"Come to the gate," Duffy said.

The man walked to the gate.

"We want Maddux," Duffy said. "We have

no interest in you. Identify Maddux to us, and you go free."

"Maddux ran out the back door," the man said. "Up San Juan . . . how you say in English? Hill."

"On foot?" Duffy said.

"Yes."

"I'll get him," Cavill said. He tossed his Winchester to Duffy, opened the gate, and grabbed a tall horse by its mane.

"Bareback?" Duffy said.

"Joseph taught me how," Cavill said.

Cavill mounted the tall horse, took hold of the mane, used it as if it were the reins, and trotted the horse out of the corral. Then he broke the horse into a full run.

"You taught him that?" Duffy said.

"I did," Goodluck said.

"You never taught me," Duffy said.

"Try staying home more," Goodluck said.

Cavill raced the horse past the house to the hill and started up it. Away from the fire, his night vision was keen.

The horse was fast. Halfway up the hill, Cavill spotted Maddux in the moonlight. He was gasping, faltering badly.

"C'mon, c'mon," Cavill said and tugged on the mane to increase the horse's speed.

Maddux heard the horse approaching behind him and tried to run faster, but he was spent, fell to his knees, and gasped for air.

Cavill caught up to Maddux, who had stated to crawl, and rode the horse in a circle around him.

"Crawl on your belly like the worm you are," Cavill shouted.

Maddux got onto his knees and looked up at Cavill.

Cavill rode the horse around Maddux and pulled the horse to the left, knocking Maddux onto his back.

"You sold human beings into slavery for profit," Cavill said and had the horse nudge Maddux again.

"Please," Maddux cried.

"That's it. You beg," Cavill said and dismounted.

"I have money," Maddux said. "Lots of money."

"Money won't do you a bit of good where you're going," Cavill said. "You sold human beings into a lifetime of misery, and then you ran like a coward when the war broke out. You sell children like they were cattle and you had the man I respected the most killed because he found out about you."

Cavill pulled his Colt revolver and cocked it.

Maddux started to cry openly. "Please

don't kill me," he said.

"I wonder how many people said the same thing when they were in your hands," Cavill said.

"All the money I have, it's yours," Maddux said.

Cavill put the Colt against Maddux's forehead.

"No, please don't kill me," Maddux cried and flopped onto his stomach.

Cavill closed his eyes for a moment. When he opened them, Maddux was crawling away on his stomach.

Cavill de-cocked the Colt and holstered it. Then he grabbed Maddux by the shirt and lifted him to his feet.

"Walk," Cavill said.

"So you men are hired just to protect Maddux when he's in Cuba," Duffy said.

"Yes," the man who spoke English said. "We also take care of his tobacco fields and take care of the house and animals when he is away."

"The tobacco field we saw on the road," Goodluck said.

"It belongs to Maddux," the man said.

"Not anymore," Duffy said. "Everything Maddux owns in Cuba now belongs to you men, including these horses."

"Jim," Goodluck said.

Duffy turned and spotted Cavill atop the horse, Maddux in front of him as they walked toward the corral.

"Joseph, tell the men to saddle four horses," Duffy said. "We have a ship to catch."

ABOUT THE AUTHOR

Ethan J. Wolfe is the author of more than a dozen historical westerns, including The Illinois Detective Agency series, the Youngblood Brothers series, and the Regulator series.